The Crowfield Curse

pat walsh

Chicken House

2 Palmer Street, Frome, Somerset BA11 1DS

Text © Pat Walsh 2010
Cover illustration © David Frankland
First published in Great Britain in 2010
The Chicken House
2 Palmer Street
Frome, Somerset BA11 1DS
United Kingdom
www.doublecluck.com

Cover and interior design by Steve Wells
Typeset by Dorchester Typesetting Group Ltd
Printed and bound in Great Britain by CPI Bookmarque, CRO 4TD

The paper used in this Chicken House book is made from wood grown
in sustainable forests.

1 3 5 7 9 10 8 6 4 2

British Library Cataloguing in Publication data available.

Trade edition ISBN 978-1-906427-15-3
Booked Up edition ISBN 978-1-906427-76-4

To John, David and Kate

Chapter One

Winter 1347

William crouched behind the fallen oak tree and listened. Close by, someone or something was whimpering in pain.

'Oh, for pity's sake . . . my leg.' Soft groans, a snuffling grunt, and then, 'My leg! Oh, my leg, mylegmylegmyleg, my leeeeg . . .'

Cautiously, William got to his feet and peered over the trunk of the tree. He could not see anyone. He stared around the woodland clearing uneasily. Frost rimed the hanks of dead grass and thin branches of hazel and elder bushes. Nothing moved. The whimpering stopped and William had the uncomfortable feeling he was being watched.

'Who's there?' he called. He waited for several moments, and then called a little louder, 'Do you need help?'

There was no reply.

William climbed over the tree. He lost his footing on the icy bark and fell, landing heavily on his hands and knees.

'Kill me, why don't you?' a voice said, weak with pain and despair. 'Land on top of me and finish the job. What is one hob more or less?' The voice trailed away into a low moan.

Startled, and more than a little alarmed, William scrambled to his feet and stared around. There was a movement in the grass by his feet. He leant down to take a closer look. The first thing he saw was a pair of large green eyes, flecked through with splinters of gold. The eyes stared back at him warily. Then he saw a small, pointed face, the skin as brown as a beechnut, pointed ears that ended in tufts of reddish brown hair and a small, thin body no bigger than a cat. A long, thin tail curled and uncurled around the body. He was a creature the like of which William had never seen before.

For a few moments, William's mind went blank. He stared down into the large, watchful eyes and felt the hairs on the back of his neck hackle. This was neither animal nor man, but he could speak. What manner of creature could do that? Fear stroked a cold finger down his spine. His mouth had gone dry and his tongue stuck to the roof of his mouth. Part of him wanted to turn and run, but another part of him was rooted to the spot by curiosity.

And then William saw the blood, and the crude iron trap that gripped the creature's leg in its rusty jaws.

'Oh, no,' he breathed, horrified. 'Stay still and I'll try and free you.' Whatever the thing was, he could not leave it to suffer like that.

Pushing his fear aside, William looked around for something to prise the trap open with. He grabbed a fallen branch and carefully wedged it between the jaws, taking care not to touch the creature's injured leg. Slowly, he began to force the jaws apart. The creature gasped and, glancing down, William saw him clamp his mouth tightly shut against the pain.

'I'm sorry,' William muttered. 'It's going to hurt, but I can't help that.'

The creature nodded and closed his eyes, and seemed to brace himself for William to continue.

Watching the small pain-twisted face, William leant his weight on the branch. The rusted hinge squealed. William gritted his teeth at the noise. The creature gripped his leg with his paws and eased it out of the trap. His fur was matted with blood and the leg was twisted at an unnatural angle. William let the branch go and the trap bit into the wood, almost snapping it in two.

'Your leg is broken,' William said, 'and that cut is very deep. If you let me take you back to the abbey, Brother Snail will be able to help you.'

The creature shook his head. He rocked back and forth, keening under his breath with the pain. 'No,no,no,no.'

'But you can't even walk by yourself, and you won't last long in this cold. The abbey is not the warmest of places, but it's better than freezing to death out here and Brother Snail is skilled at bone-setting.'

The creature sat hunched on the frosty ground, his long thin arms wrapped tightly around his trembling body. The wound oozed dark blood. 'No.'

William shrugged helplessly. 'You don't really have a choice, unless you have someone else who can help you.' He looked around uncertainly. Were there more of these creatures in Foxwist Wood? And what had it called itself? A hob? 'Is there anyone?'

The hob shook his head again. 'Nobody.'

'Then it'll have to be Brother Snail at the abbey.'

'Mends hobs, does he?' The hob squinted up at

him, a pinched expression on his face. William had the feeling the creature did not greatly trust humans. '*Likes* hobs, does he?'

'I don't think he's ever met one,' William said, after a moment's thought. 'But I know he will do what he can to help you, whatever you are.'

The hob seemed to consider this. He winced as another wave of pain hit him and that seemed to help him make up his mind. 'Very well,' the creature gasped breathlessly, 'I will come with you.'

William hid the firewood he had been collecting under a low sweeping branch of the fallen tree. As soon as he had made sure the hob was in the capable hands of the abbey infirmarer, he would hurry back to retrieve it. This part of Foxwist Wood was on abbey land, and villagers from Weforde and Yagleah were not allowed to gather wood here, but that rarely stopped them. Any doubt he might have had that the villagers used the wood as their own was banished by the sight of the iron trap. They were not permitted to hunt in Foxwist either but a handful of them clearly did, safe in the certainty that Prior Ardo would not do a thing about it.

The hob could barely manage to struggle to his feet, so William picked him up and carried him.

The track to the abbey wove its way through the wood and dipped down into a shallow valley. A river meandered through low-lying flood meadows, a glint of pewter shining in the winter sun between the reed beds. On a rise of ground beside it stood the grey stone buildings of Crowfield Abbey.

The abbey was small and as poor as grave dirt. It had been William's home for a year and a half now; long enough for him to know there were few amongst the monks who would look upon the hob with anything less than deep suspicion. He would need to smuggle the creature into Brother Snail's workshop without being seen. Luckily, as he crossed the bridge over the river, the bell for tierce clanged out clear and sharp, calling the monks to the church. Tierce, closely following High Mass, would be short, with just a few psalms sung, and immediately afterwards, the monks would file into the chapter house to deal with the matters of the day. That would keep them safely out of the way and busy for a goodly while, long enough for William to settle the injured creature in the workshop and hurry back to Foxwist to collect the firewood.

They reached the gatehouse and William pushed open the wicket door to one side of the main gate. He peered around the edge of the door and saw that the yard between the gatehouse and the kitchen was empty, except for a few hens scraping about on the frozen mud. Wrapping a corner of his jacket around the hob, William hurried over to the kitchen door, slipping and skidding on the icy puddles, and let himself in.

So far so good; as he had hoped, there was nobody around. The kitchen was empty. It would be a while yet before Brother Martin started to bake the day's bread and prepare the pottage for dinner.

The thought of food, even Brother Martin's vegetable pottage, made William's mouth water. Hunger rarely left him and he often daydreamed about the hare stew and mutton broth his mother used to cook, before a fire at the mill had claimed the lives of his parents and younger brother and sister. Quickly, he put the memory of that terrible night out of his thoughts. His old life had died in the fire with his family and now he had to make the best of this new life. It wasn't what he would have chosen for himself, but at least he had a roof over his head and food in his belly and for now, that was enough.

A fire burned on the hearth in the middle of the room, directly below the soot-blackened smoke hole in the roof. The kitchen was one of only a couple of rooms in the whole abbey that had a fire, and it was never allowed to go out. William paused beside it for a moment, wishing he could stay longer, but he could not risk the hob being discovered. A broken leg would be the least of his worries if Brother Martin caught sight of him.

William opened the door to the cloister and listened. The sound of singing came from the church, thin and distant; too few voices lost in the huge stone emptiness of the abbey church. He hurried along the cloister alley to the narrow passage between the church and the chapter house, and out into the monks' graveyard. A path led away to his right, to the vegetable garden and the dovecot. Beyond it, fringed by reeds, was the abbey fishpond, and to one side of that, half hidden beneath the branches of a blackthorn tree, stood a small reed-thatched timber hut. It was here that Brother Snail prepared potions and salves from the plants he grew in the abbey garden and gathered in the fields and woods around the abbey.

Peter Borowe, Crowfield's only lay brother, was busy pulling up leeks in the vegetable garden, working them loose from the frozen earth with a hoe and throwing them into a nearby basket. He straightened up and waved when he saw William. His face and hands were red from the cold. He leant his elbow on the top of the hoe and blew into his cupped fingers to warm them.

William swore under his breath, but he waved back as he made his way quickly along the path to the door of the hut. He lifted the latch and went inside, closing and bolting the door behind him.

He was reasonably sure Peter would not follow him, but with Peter, you could never be entirely certain what he would do. A grown man of twenty years, he had the simplicity and mind of a child. The world he lived in was very different to the real world around him and sometimes he forgot what he was supposed to be doing. He liked William because he was one of the few people at the abbey who took the time to sit and talk to him, but right now that was the last thing William wanted.

'You should be safe here,' William said, setting the hob down carefully beside the stone-lined fire pit in the middle of the floor. The fire was covered with a large pottery *couvre-feu*, a domed lid with holes poked through it, to stop stray sparks landing on the wooden floor or a basket or sack and setting fire to the hut.

William wrapped a rag around the handle on top of the lid and lifted it aside. He added a few pieces of wood to the embers.

'Can I trust you to watch the fire,' William asked, 'while I go back and fetch the wood? I won't be long. You can rest here in the warm.'

The hob nodded and looked around, his eyes full of curiosity in spite of his pain. 'I will watch your fire. Where is the snail brother? The one you said would help?'

'In church, for tierce.'

The hob frowned. 'What is a tierce?'

'It's not a what, it's a when. It's one of the times during the day when the monks go to the church to pray and sing.'

The hob slowly eased his leg into a more comfortable position. 'Why?'

William was a little startled by the question. It was not something he had ever thought about. He had always simply accepted the monks' routine of prayer and work. 'That's just what they do. They're monks,' he added with a shrug, as if that explained everything. It clearly didn't, not to the hob anyway.

'Are they singing because they are happy?'

'I suppose so, in a way. They're praising God.'

'And they can only do that by singing?' The hob put his head on one side and gazed up at William.

'Of course not,' William said. 'They pray and work and copy holy books with writing and small pictures in them.'

'That is what their god wants them to do for him?' The creature sounded surprised. He was quiet for a moment. 'What does he do with all the books?'

William felt a flicker of impatience. He had more than enough work of his own waiting for him; he did not have time to try and explain things to the hob that he did not fully understand himself. 'The monks don't give the books to God, and before you ask anything else, I have to go. Wait here and don't touch anything. I will be back as quickly as I can.'

The hob lay down on its side and curled its tail over its body. 'Very well.'

William hesitated for a couple of moments. Was it safe to leave the creature here? What if Peter came in unexpectedly and startled it? What would it do?

'It might be a good idea, if anyone comes to the hut, for you to hide,' he suggested.

'Humans cannot usually see me,' the hob said, 'unless I choose to let them, or if they have the Sight.' The creature closed his eyes. William felt a flicker of worry. The hob was in terrible pain and he had lost a lot of blood. What if he died before Brother Snail could do anything to help him?

Well, everything dies, sooner or later, William thought, a bleakness of spirit wrapping itself around him like a fog. When your time came, that was that. It was just the way of things.

William pulled up his hood, tucking the long strands of his untidy blond hair inside, and walked to the door. What had started out as an ordinary November day had taken a very strange turn indeed. He just hoped he hadn't made a mistake in bringing the creature to the abbey.

Chapter Two

William left the hut and set off back to the abbey. Peter looked up hopefully as he passed by, but William did not stop to talk. He did not have time. He merely waved and broke into a run, heading for the passageway into the cloister.

The monks had left the church and were now in the chapter house. William heard Prior Ardo's voice as he passed the door, low and monotonous, reading the day's chapter from St Benedict's Rule. According to Brother Snail, it sometimes took an effort of will to stay awake during one of Prior Ardo's readings. 'I think God sent the prior to us to test our patience and our devotion to Him,' Snail had once told William, a sly twinkle in his eye. 'And I fear we don't always do too well.'

William jogged back to Foxwist. He reached the

fallen tree and was relieved to find the bundle of firewood still hidden beneath the branch. He hefted it onto his back, twisting his fingers through the hemp rope he had tied it with and turned to go, but then he paused. The trap. He could not leave it here to be used to maim or kill some other hapless creature.

William lowered the firewood again, twisting his body to let it drop from his back and grunting with the effort.

The trap lay where he had left it, its jaws still gripping the branch he'd forced it open with. For a few moments William wondered what to do with it. If he hid the trap, someone might find it and use it again. He could not bury it because the ground was frozen as hard as stone. He needed to get rid of it altogether.

An idea suddenly occurred to him. There was one place where the trap would be safely out of reach for good, one place nobody would go anywhere near, day or night: the Whistling Hollow. Even the track from Yagleah to Weforde looped out of its way to avoid it.

William hesitated for a few moments. His heart beat a little more quickly with the first stirrings of fear. What if the stories he had heard about the Whistling Hollow were true? What if he heard the strange whistling sound that local people believed

14

called up the Wild Hunt? It was all too easy to imagine the pack of ghostly hounds, red eyes glowing, jaws gaping, as they chased terrified victims through the wood, to tear their immortal souls from their bodies and carry them off to hell.

William swallowed a couple of times and licked his dry lips. It would only take a moment to throw the trap into the pool at the bottom of the Hollow. Then he would make a run for the safety of the abbey as if all the demons in hell were hard on his heels. Did he have the courage to do it? He glanced down at the trap and saw the dried blood and tufts of brown fur caught between the iron jaws. He felt a surge of anger and decided he had no other choice.

He picked up the trap and held it cradled awkwardly against his chest. It was heavy and the iron was painfully cold. The trap was crudely made but effective. As far as William could work out, an animal only had to step on a thin iron plate to release the jaws. Then the saw-toothed edges would clamp shut, hard and fast, cutting through flesh and snapping bone. The animal would have no hope of freeing itself, and the trap would be a dead weight on its injured limb, making escape virtually impossible. Pain and loss of blood would soon leave the creature weak and helpless. William felt the sting of angry tears and blinked them away. To do that to a living creature was too cruel for words.

William knew where the Hollow was, though he had never seen it for himself. The first time he had gone to Weforde with Brother Gabriel, to sell the abbey's surplus vegetables at the Wednesday market, the plump little monk had warned him never to venture near it. The monk had crossed himself several times and prayed aloud until they were safely past the dense thicket of bushes and holly trees that hid the Hollow from the track.

'This is an unholy place, boy,' Brother Gabriel had told him. 'Step off the track between the Boundary Oak and the sighting stone above Weforde Brook and you'll be lost. The devil himself walks the woods hereabouts and he is always on the lookout for Christian souls.'

William had wondered what was to stop the devil from merely walking out onto the track and helping himself to the souls there.

'And if you hear whistling in this part of the wood,' the monk added, giving William a hard stare, 'run, boy, and don't look back.'

William set off along the track. The sharp edges of

the trap dug into his arms and he had to stop every now and then to shift it to a more comfortable position. Before long, he reached the huge old Boundary Oak, marking the westernmost limit of abbey lands. Beyond it, the track turned sharply away to the left. Small scraps of rag were tied to the branches of nearby trees and bushes as a warning to unwary travellers not to stray from the track, on peril of their souls.

William paused to take a few deep, steadying breaths before pushing his way through the tangled branches of a hazel thicket. He glanced around all the time, alert for the first hint of danger. Fallen branches littered the ground, good kindling for the most part, but left to rot where they fell. It seemed that none of the locals were desperate enough for firewood to risk coming here.

Holly bushes grew abundantly in this part of Foxwist. Clusters of scarlet berries weighed down the branches. William wondered why they hadn't been picked clean by birds. Now that he thought about it, he noticed there *were* no birds. In the distance he could hear crows cawing, but close by the wood was silent. No bird song, no small rustlings from some animal in the undergrowth, nothing to disturb the absolute stillness. But it was not a peaceful silence. It wrapped itself around William like a cold shadow and he shivered. He quickened his pace, not wanting to stay there a moment longer than he had to.

An ancient yew tree stood like a dark-cloaked sentinel in the gloom, guarding the wood. Fear twisted in the pit of William's stomach. The atmosphere around him had changed subtly. He felt as if something was watching him with baleful, hostile eyes.

William couldn't turn back now. The trap seemed to carry with it the spirits of the creatures that had died in its grip. William was determined that it would never harm another animal. It would lie in the water at the bottom of the Hollow and rust away to nothing.

A breeze swayed through the undergrowth. 'There will be other traps, other deaths,' it seemed to whisper.

William's heart leaped in fear and he stared around, wide-eyed and terrified. There was nobody there. He could not be sure if he had really heard the words, or if they had been inside his head. In spite of that, the feeling of being watched grew stronger by the moment. It took every shred of courage he could muster to force himself to start walking forward again.

Why didn't I just take the trap back to the abbey? he

thought. *What made me think coming here was a good idea?*

On the far side of the yew, the ground sloped downhill. The scrub thinned, and he could see a shallow, marshy pool of water at the bottom of the slope. This was the Hollow. He knew it, he could *feel* it.

It was noticeably colder now. William's breath clouded on the still air. Frost silvered the reeds around the pool and the water's edge was frozen over with a crust of blue-white ice, leaving just a circle of dark water in the middle.

Hesitantly, William made his way towards the pool. His hands were clammy, making it awkward to keep hold of the trap. He could feel sweat trickle between his shoulder blades. His heart seemed to be trying to beat its way out of his chest, making it difficult to breathe. *Doing the right thing is not always the easy choice*, he thought grimly.

An old hazel tree grew on the edge of the pool and spread its branches out over the water. There were several moss-covered stones beneath its twisted roots. Water trickled between them.

What magic stopped the spring from freezing over in the middle of November, when the rest of the land was held tightly in winter's bleak grip?

The centre of the pool was a black mirror that reflected an upside-down world. The water might have been knee-deep, or it might have been bottomless, there was no way of knowing, but William had the oddest feeling that if he fell into the water, he would find himself sinking down into that shadowy otherworld.

He did not like this place, not one little bit. It did not want him here, either. He was an intruder, an outsider. If he stayed much longer, it would make him wish he hadn't.

With a huge effort, William threw the trap as hard as he could, out over the ice, towards the dark heart of the pool. There was a loud splash as it hit the water and sank beneath the surface.

He stepped back from the edge and watched the ripples die away. The water became still again. A movement of cold air touched his cheek and he turned quickly, grabbing a branch of the hazel tree to stop himself from falling backwards onto the icy margin of the pool. For a heart-stopping moment, he had the feeling that someone was standing close by. He could not see anything but he felt a presence so strongly he could almost touch it.

'This will not be forgotten.' The whispered words

had no more substance than a breath of wind through branches.

William went hot and cold with terror. Forcing his shaking legs to move, he turned and ran.

Chapter Three

Willinm left the bundle of firewood in the woodshed near the barn. He could hear Brother Martin, the abbey cook, clattering about and swearing in the cellarium next to the kitchen and he quickened his step. If the monk caught sight of him, he would be trapped in the kitchen for the rest of the morning, cutting up vegetables for dinner, and he would not get a chance to ask Brother Snail to help the hob.

William hurried out into the cloister alley. Through one of the large arched openings overlooking the cloister garth, he saw Brother Snail, digging in a herb bed below the bare branches of a walnut tree. He was thirty-one years old and the youngest monk at the abbey, though at first glance he did not look it. He was small and thin, with pale skin stretched tightly across his bones, and a hunched back. His real name was

Thomas, but he had been known as Snail ever since his spine had begun to curve and set like stone when he was fourteen years old, the same age as William was now. He worked slowly, using the light wooden spade Edgar, the carpenter in Yagleah, had made especially for him.

William watched the little monk for a couple of moments and could almost feel his pain with each slow stab of the spade. If William had time later, in between his other daily tasks, he would help with the digging. What would take Brother Snail most of the day to do, William could finish in an hour.

William glanced around. Two monks sat at their desks in the north walk of the cloister, close to the door into the church. In spite of the cold numbing their fingers, they were engrossed in their work, copying the psalter loaned to them for the purpose by Sir Robert de Tovei of Weforde, and they took no notice of William.

He made his way over to Brother Snail, his feet crunching on the gravel brought up from the river to cover the narrow pathways between the herb beds.

'Will,' the monk said, looking sideways and up at him with a smile. 'Shouldn't you be busy in the kitchen?'

'I'll go there soon,' William said, 'but first I need your help with something.'

Brother Snail looked a little surprised but he leant on the handle of his spade and nodded. 'Very well. What is it?'

William hesitated for a moment. 'I rescued a creature from a trap in Foxwist Wood. He's badly injured. Can you come and look at him?'

The monk frowned and wiped the earth from his hands on his faded and much-patched black habit. 'A trap!' he said angrily. 'Not again! I will speak to Abbot Simon about this.' He stopped and his mouth hardened into a straight line. He had spoken without thinking.

William knew Brother Snail would not talk to the abbot about the trap. What would be the use? Everybody knew Abbot Simon was hanging onto life by a thread and he no longer knew where or who he was. Traps in Foxwist would mean nothing to him.

'I will speak to Prior Ardo,' Snail said quietly. Ardo might be sour and humourless, but he had taken over the running of the abbey and was doing his best to keep it on the right side of hunger and poverty. 'Where is it, this animal of yours? And what is it? A hare? A fox?'

William took a deep breath and said, 'Neither. It's not any kind of animal, it's a hob.'

The monk stared at him for several moments, a startled expression on his face. 'A hob?' he said at last. 'Are you sure, Will? A *hob*?'

William nodded and watched the monk anxiously. Had he made a mistake in trusting Brother Snail? Would he consider the hob to be a creature of the devil, not to be tolerated on holy ground?

'And how do you know that it's a hob?'

'Because he told me he was,' William said cautiously.

'I see.' There was a thoughtful expression in Brother Snail's light blue eyes. 'There used to be hobmen in Foxwist and up on Gremanhil, according to the old stories,' the monk said, keeping his voice low and glancing over at the two monks busy at their desks, 'but I thought they had long since gone. What are his injuries?'

William felt a surge of relief. Brother Snail believed him, and more importantly, he was not crossing himself and calling down the wrath of God on William's head for daring to bring such a creature to the abbey. That was definitely a good sign. 'A broken leg, a deep wound, and he has lost a lot of blood.'

'Where is he now?'

'In your workshop.'

'Come with me, Will. If anyone asks, you are helping me with something urgent, but don't mention the hob.' The monk set off along the path with surprising speed and a curious sideways gait. William hurried after him.

'Is the trap still in the wood?' Brother Snail asked as they left the abbey behind and headed across the vegetable garden towards the hut. Peter Borowe and his basket of vegetables had gone.

'No. I got rid of it,' William said. 'I took it to the Whistling Hollow and threw it into the pool.'

Snail stopped abruptly. William almost collided with him.

'You did *what*?' the monk said, turning to stare up at him with a worried frown. 'Don't you know how dangerous it is to go anywhere near the Hollow, William? Haven't you been warned often enough?'

William felt hot colour rise to his cheeks. 'I wanted to make sure nobody would ever be able to use the trap again. It seemed the best way to do it.'

'And you don't think whoever set the trap has others? Or that you could have brought it here and hidden it in a shed?'

26

William shrugged one shoulder and looked away. 'I didn't come to any harm,' he muttered.

'Maybe so, this time,' Snail said, setting off again, 'but the local people avoid that place for a very good reason, Will, and you were foolish to disregard the warnings.' The monk was quiet for a moment, then asked, 'Did you see or hear anything while you were there?'

'I . . . I'm not sure,' William said hesitantly. The monk stopped again and turned to look him, head to one side, looking for all the world like a small and inquisitive bird. He tucked his thin hands into the sleeves of his habit and waited for William to continue.

'I thought I heard a voice,' William began. He told the monk what had happened and how he had felt he was being watched. It seemed little enough now, in familiar everyday surroundings, but fear still shadowed his mind.

The monk frowned. There was a look in his eyes that made William wonder if he knew more about the Hollow than he was saying.

'Have you ever been there?' William asked, watching the monk's face closely.

Snail did not reply at first. He gazed into the

distance and seemed troubled. At last, he looked back at William. 'Many years ago, not long after I came to live at Crowfield, I had cause to go to Weforde,' he said. 'Some matter of a message from the abbot to Sir Robert. I stopped to look for plants along the way and forgot the time. When I realised I wouldn't have time to deliver the message and get back to the abbey before dark, I did a foolish thing. I took a short cut through the woods. My path took me down into the Hollow.' The monk stopped and William saw him shiver. It might simply have been the cold, but William had the feeling it was more than that.

'It was a wet autumn day and the ground was boggy near the pool. There was a tree growing out over the water.'

William nodded. 'Above the spring, a hazel tree.'

Snail looked surprised, as if he hadn't expected William to have noticed such a detail. 'Yes, that's right. Its leaves had turned colour and it looked as if someone had hung gold coins from every branch and twig. I remember it so clearly, because the leaves in the rest of the wood were a dull brown, and the hazel tree shone like a beacon in the gloom.' He paused for a moment and smiled faintly at the memory. Then his eyes clouded again. 'I looked back when I reached the far side of the Hollow. I saw something by the pool. It was just a misty shape, but I had the feeling it was watching me. I have never been so frightened of anything in my whole life, Will. I had the distinct feeling I should not have been there and that I was not welcome.'

William nodded. 'That's what I felt too. What did you do?'

Snail smiled thinly. 'I ran.'

William grinned. 'Me too.'

'And I never took a short cut through the woods again,' Brother Snail finished. 'And neither should you. Stay away from the Hollow, Will. You might not be so lucky next time.'

'Lucky?' William repeated, puzzled.

'You're still alive.' Snail turned and set off again, shuffling along, his head bowed between humped shoulders. It was hard to imagine him as a young man, still able to run.

'Have people died there?' William asked in alarm.

'All I know is that people have sometimes gone missing in Foxwist. Maybe they're dead, maybe not, but whatever the truth of it is, I think you had a narrow escape, Will. Be grateful for that and don't go near the Hollow again.'

'The figure you saw, was it a ghost, do you think?' William asked, falling into step beside the monk.

'I doubt it.'

'Oh? What was it, then?'

'Something as old as the woods and the hills,' the monk said quietly, turning to gaze across the river, towards Foxwist. 'I believe it was here long before the abbey and Weforde and Yagleah, and will still be here long after they've gone. I don't have a name for it, Will, but I believe it was the spirit of the place.'

William shivered. He did not realise places could have spirits. He glanced around uneasily. The world was beginning to feel far stranger and more dangerous than he had ever imagined. His life growing up in the mill at Iwele had been much simpler than his life at the abbey.

They reached the workshop and Snail lifted the latch. 'Perhaps the hob will be able to tell me what it really was,' he said with a quick smile at William.

'If he's still alive,' William said grimly.

'Well, let's find out, shall we?'

Chapter Four

Brother Snail kept a lantern on a shelf inside the door, along with a tinderbox and a couple of spare tallow candles. He lit the stub of candle inside the lantern and looked around the workshop. 'Where is he, then, this hob of yours?'

It was some moments before William spotted the creature, huddled between a basket of logs and the hut wall. 'Over there.'

Snail frowned as he peered into the gloom. 'Where?'

William crouched down beside the basket and held out a hand to the hob. The creature shuffled forward awkwardly and grabbed William's fingers. As gently as he could, William helped the hob out of its hiding place.

The creature seemed weaker now. There was a trail of blood on the floor where it dragged its leg. William heard Brother Snail gasp. He glanced over his shoulder. The monk was staring down at the injured creature, his eyes wide with shock. It seemed the monk hadn't fully believed in hobs until that moment.

'Can you help him?' William asked anxiously.

'I will try,' Snail said, a slight tremor in his voice. 'Bring him to the table, Will.' He rolled up his sleeves and poured water from the pail by the door into a bowl.

William did as he was told. He cleared a space amongst the pots, bowls and bundles of dried plants, and settled the hob on the scrubbed oak boards. The thin fingered paws held tightly to William's hand and the small body trembled. William stroked the fur on its back to try and reassure it. The hob tensed. William had the feeling it didn't like being touched like this. He lowered his hand and saw the hob relax a little.

Snail examined the hob's leg, his fingers careful and gentle as they wiped the blood from its fur with a rag dipped in the water. 'The break is clean. The trap snapped the bone but didn't crush it into pieces, which is a good thing,' he said, glancing at the hob. 'It should mend and be as good as new. I'll clean the wound and splint the leg, and then I'll mix you a caudle to ease the pain. You will need to rest until the bone heals.' He dried his hands on a clean corner of the rag and turned away to fetch what he would need to treat the hob. 'You are welcome to stay here at the abbey until you are well enough to go back to the woods.'

The hob looked up at William. Its face was drawn and its eyes shadowed with suspicion. It clearly did not trust people, and who could blame it?

'It might be for the best,' William said. 'You can't fend for yourself if you can't walk.'

'Hobs and men have never been friends,' the hob said, looking from William to Brother Snail. 'Sometimes men let us live in their homes, tend their animals and clean their pots, but they do not like us or trust us. Mostly they do not even believe in us. Why should you be any different?'

'Well, for a start,' Brother Snail said, raising his eyebrows, 'I believe in you, seeing as you're sitting there in front of me. And I have no reason to dislike or distrust you, unless you give me cause to do so. Is that good enough for you?'

The hob nodded slowly.

'Good,' the monk said briskly. 'Now I'll prepare that caudle. William, you have work to do in the kitchen. You can come by and see our patient later.'

William opened his mouth to argue, but closed it again. Brother Snail was right. He should be in the kitchen, chopping vegetables.

'Hurry along then,' Snail said, glancing at him with a smile, as if understanding his reluctance to leave the hut.

William walked to the door. He paused with his hand on the latch and looked back at the hob. 'What's your name?'

The hob's eyes narrowed and it looked away. 'I will not tell you.'

'Why not?' William asked in surprise.

The hob did not reply.

Brother Snail smiled slightly and glanced at William. 'He can't tell you, because if he does, it will give you power over him. Fay folk never tell humans their names, ever, unless they are tricked into doing so.'

The hob continued to stare at the wall, deter-minedly silent.

'So what are we meant to call you?' William asked.

The hob raised one shoulder in a shrug.

'We'll call you Brother Walter,' Snail said with a gleam in his eyes. 'Would that suit you?'

The hob turned and regarded the monk thoughtfully for several moments, and then it nodded. 'It will do.'

'That's settled, then,' Snail said, 'Brother Walter it is.'

William grinned. 'That'll please Prior Ardo and the other monks.'

'They don't need to know,' Snail said firmly. 'Now, get back to your work, Will, before Brother Martin comes looking for you.'

William did not need to be told again. It was very unwise to get on the wrong side of the abbey's cook, an old soldier with one eye and a foul temper.

'I'll be back before dinner,' he said, opening the door.

The monk nodded. 'Bring some food with you for Brother Walter.'

William pulled a face. The most he could hope to smuggle out of the kitchen was a bit of bread and a bowl of Brother Martin's vegetable pottage.

As if the hob had not already suffered enough for one day.

'Yer late,' Brother Martin growled, his one brown eye fixing William with a steely glare. 'Where you bin?'

'Helping Brother Snail,' William said, picking up

the basket of vegetables that Peter Borowe had delivered to the kitchen. He carried it over to the table and dumped it down beside a pail of water. Rolling up his sleeves, he started to pull the leaves off a cabbage and drop them into the water. He knew the routine; he had done it almost every day since he'd come to live at Crowfield. Peel, wash and chop cabbage, carrots and leeks, a few onions and anything else the lay brother had managed to scavenge from the fields and woods around the abbey. Today there were three small carp from the abbey fishpond to add to the vegetables. William frowned down at them. At least one of them looked as if it had died of old age. They would do little more than add some flavour to the pottage, and if the smell was anything to go by, it was not going to be pleasant.

Brother Martin was making maslin bread for the main meal of the day, using a mixture of coarse dark rye and wheat flour. Soft white wheat bread was unheard of at Crowfield. It was just one more reminder, not that it was needed, of how frugally the monks lived.

Brother Martin had already been at the cider, it seemed. He made it himself from the apples growing in the abbey orchard, and it was strong enough to kill a horse. His cheeks were mottled dark red and he muttered to himself as he pounded the dough, his heavy fists pummelling it with a savagery that was frightening to watch. William eyed him warily. The stockily built monk with his scarred face and leathery skin seemed to be permanently full of rage, but at what or whom, William had never found out. You could not hold a conversation with Brother Martin; he spoke only to snap orders or pour scathing contempt on William's efforts in the kitchen. Sometimes he seemed to forget he was no longer a soldier and had on several occasions threatened to tie William to a post and have him flogged.

'As if we ain't enough damned work to do without *guests* dragging their stinking carcasses to the abbey gates and living off us like leeches,' the monk spat, knuckles thumping the dough. 'Cook meat for 'em, Brother Martin, make pretty food and fine white bread for 'em, Brother Martin, wipe their arses for 'em, Brother Martin,' he sneered. He turned to scowl at William. 'Get that lot finished and then go and help that idle layabout Borowe to muck out the guest chambers.'

William stared at him in astonishment. Here was an unexpected piece of news, guests coming to the abbey. Who were they? How long did they intend to stay? From what Brother Snail had told him, it was many years since anyone had stayed at Crowfield. Why would they? There were a couple of larger, richer abbeys within a couple of day's ride of Crowfield, both far more suited to the needs of hungry and weary travellers. All he could think was that the guests, whoever they were, had no idea what they were letting themselves in for.

Brother Martin took a short-bladed knife from his belt and slashed the dough into smaller pieces, ready to shape into loaves and bake in the oven in the yard. 'Mark my words, soldier,' he said suddenly, pointing the knife blade at William, 'there will be trouble. Strangers in the camp, not good. Not good at all, you wait and see.'

It was a relief when the last of the vegetables was cut up and added to the cauldron hanging over the fire and William could escape from the kitchen.

Chapter Five

The guest chambers were on the west side of the cloister, below the abbot's chamber. The door stood open and two straw mattresses and a pile of bedding lay on the ground nearby. William could hear something heavy being dragged across the stone-flagged floor inside.

He stood in the doorway for a moment to look around. He had never been into any of the rooms on this side of the cloister before. He had no reason to go up to the abbot's chambers, and the rooms below them were kept locked. The abbey had been built to house many more monks than the eleven it did today and half of its rooms were empty.

The guest chambers consisted of two rooms: a large chamber with a vaulted ceiling supported on two rows of squat stone pillars, and a small room tucked between the end wall of the chamber and the nave wall of the church. A second door led out to the yard, but it was locked and Peter did not have the key. There were three windows, just narrow slits high up on the wall overlooking the yard. They were covered with wooden shutters that kept out the rain, snow and cold winds. They also kept out the grey winter daylight. The single rushlight in the iron bracket near the door barely troubled the shadows.

An indistinct shape moved between the pillars and stepped into the patch of light by the open doorway. It was Peter Borowe, and he smiled when he saw William, his face bright with a child-like pleasure.

'Will!' he said with obvious delight. 'Are you here to help me?'

William nodded and smiled in return. 'I am. What do you want me to do first?'

'We have to move all the old, broken things out of here and burn them in the yard, Prior Ardo says. Then we brush the floor and put down clean rushes, scrub the table and chairs, and make up two beds.' Peter spoke slowly and carefully, marking each task by gripping the outstretched fingers of one hand in turn. His voice was thick, with a slight lisp, as if his tongue was too big for his mouth. There was an earnest expression on his broad, blunt-featured face as he tried to remember exactly what it was that the prior had told him. William waited patiently for him to finish.

'We have to bring more rushlights and ask Brother Snail for a wax candle from his store cupboard, and . . .' he hesitated and there was a look of panic in his eyes as he struggled to recall the next thing on his list of tasks.

'Fetch firewood?' William suggested.

Relief flooded Peter's face. 'Yes, yes! That was it! A fire. Clean the hearth and lay the fire.'

'We'd better make a start, then,' William said, peering around with a grimace. The room had been used for storage over the years and the cold air smelled musty and stale. Everything was covered in a thick layer of dust that rose in clouds and caught in their throats and made them cough. A pile of old straw mattresses in one corner had been chewed to shreds by rats and stank to high Heaven. Small quick bodies scurried away into the shadows as soon as William pulled the first mattress from the pile and dragged it to the door.

Between them, William and Peter hauled the mattresses out into the cloister, and from there through the kitchen and out into the yard. To

William's relief, Brother Martin was not around to see the trail of filthy straw that followed them across the floor. With luck, he would get it swept up before the cook came back. It was either that or be on the receiving end of a thump from the monk's hard fist.

Before too long, all the discarded furniture was piled up in the middle of the yard, well away from the barn and outbuildings, ready for burning. The two best beds were left in the chamber, along with a table and two plain oak chairs. The furniture had seen better days but it was all the abbey had to offer and would have to do.

William fetched a couple of birch-twig brooms from the store room next to the kitchen and gave one to Peter. Starting against the end wall of the guest chamber, they swept the stone-paved floor, until a pile of dusty straw and worm-eaten, powdery wood lay in the doorway. They swept the room a second time, and then scraped up the pile with a shovel and tipped it into a couple of wooden pails, which they emptied onto the midden in the yard.

William fetched water from the well and washed down the furniture, while Peter draped the new mattresses over the chairs and beat them with Brother Martin's bread shovel to even out the lumps of straw.

Between them, they made up the beds and arranged the furniture against the walls.

In the dim, dusty light, the room looked cavernous and bare. The huge fireplace was a gloomy cave set deep into the end wall of the room. A draught moaned up and down the chimney. Cold struck up from the floor and the pillars seemed to William to be the trunks of stone trees, whose branches disappeared into the darkness of the arched roof.

He looked up and wondered at the skill of the stonemasons who had built the abbey. To fashion curving ribs that hung high overhead, and carve leaves and branches into stone, was as close to magic as it was possible to get. William spent secret moments in the church and cloister peering at the tiny details hidden in the carvings that decorated the stonework: animals, plants and birds, the faces of people and demons and angels, the once-bright colours with which they had been painted now faded and dulled with time. It was a reflection of Heaven and Earth, turned to stone.

Peter swept the hearth while William went to fetch firewood from the woodshed. He was stacking logs into a basket when he heard voices outside in the yard. He looked through the doorway and saw Prior Ardo and Brother Gabriel standing by the open abbey gate, with a man William recognised as Edgar the carpenter, a freeman from Yagleah. He saw him most market days at Weforde, selling the wooden buckets and bowls he made. Edgar seemed agitated and his raised voice carried on the still cold air.

'He were arskin' questins, lots on 'em, and he *knew*, I swear it, Prior, he *knew*.' The man glanced over his shoulder, as if worried he was being watched or overheard. 'He arsked 'bout the angel. He knew all about it, 'bout it bein' dead and buried . . .'

The man got no further.

'Be silent!' Prior Ardo hissed angrily, grabbing the man's arm with his long bony fingers. 'Come with me.'

Between them, Ardo and Gabriel quickly bundled the man across the yard and out of sight around the corner of the west range. Whatever business the carpenter had with the abbey, the monks were clearly anxious for it to remain private.

An angel, dead and buried?

But that's blasphemy, surely? William thought, puzzled and troubled by what he had just witnessed. How could an angel die? And what had it to do with the monks of Crowfield Abbey?

William was in a thoughtful mood for the rest of

the day as he went about his chores. If Peter noticed, it did not seem to trouble him, and he chattered on with his usual cheerfulness about anything and nothing.

As soon as the monks had filed into the church for nones, the last service before dinner, William filled a bowl with pottage for the hob and put it carefully in a flat-bottomed basket. He took a small loaf from the rows of newly baked maslin cooling on the table and put that in the basket too. He fervently hoped that Brother Martin had not counted them. There would be trouble if William was caught stealing and he could not imagine trying to explain to Prior Ardo what he had wanted the loaf for. The best he could hope for was a sound beating. The worst was to be thrown out of the abbey and left to fend for himself, and that did not bear thinking about in the middle of winter.

William lit a stub of tallow candle from the fire and put it inside the battered old iron lantern that was kept on a hook by the yard door, and left the kitchen.

The afternoon was fading into a freezing dusk and a thin layer of mist lay over the river and flood meadows. A half moon rose over Foxwist Wood and a single star shone in the sky above the rounded hump of Gremanhil, beyond the abbey's East Field. Nothing

45

disturbed the stillness and the only sound was the rasp of William's boots on the icy ground.

It had been a strange day, all in all. William was not sure what disturbed him the most – finding the hob, the voice he had heard in the Whistling Hollow, or the snatch of conversation he had overheard between the villager and the monks. It was if the everyday world had slipped to one side and he'd glimpsed something else, something much darker and harder to understand.

William paused for a moment outside the workshop door and looked around to make sure nobody had followed him from the abbey. Quite why anyone would, he didn't know, but a nagging feeling that he was being watched had been growing since he left the safety of the abbey kitchen. There was still just enough light to see that the vegetable garden and the East Field were empty.

But *something* was out there, hidden in the dusk, watching him, he was certain of it. His skin prickled uneasily as he stared across the river towards the woods and imagined someone looking back at him.

Pulling his jacket more closely around his shivering body, he lifted the latch and stepped inside the hut.

Chapter Six

William put the lantern on the table and opened the small shutter in its front. The hob was curled up asleep on a pile of old, clean rags in a basket by the fire. The *couvre-feu* lay on the floor nearby. The embers in the fire-pit glowed and small flames flickered briefly every now and then. The hob's reddish fur glinted russet-gold in the fire-light and his tail was wrapped neatly around his small body.

William knelt beside the basket and touched the hob's shoulder gently to wake him. The hob stirred and chittered softly in his sleep. William added a couple of branches to the fire and flames licked the dry wood. He set the pottage in a corner of the fire-pit to keep warm and put the loaf of bread on a hearth stone.

'Brother Walter?' he said, shaking the hob again. 'Are you hungry? I've brought some food.'

Slowly, sleepily, the hob stretched and eased his body into a more comfortable position. His bandaged leg stuck out awkwardly and he winced as he tried to move it. The green eyes opened and the hob stared blankly at William, as if, for the moment, he had forgotten where he was.

'Are you hungry?' William repeated.

The hob nodded and worked himself up into a sitting position, with his injured leg stretched out in front of him.

William looked around for a spoon. He found one on the table, and stirred the pottage with it.

'What do you usually eat?' he asked curiously, wrapping the warm pot in a rag and handing the pot and spoon to the hob.

The hob examined the spoon for a couple of moments, and then put it on the floor. 'Nuts, berries, leaves.' He sniffed the pottage and wrinkled his nose. He glanced up at William and then took a cautious sip from the pot. 'Not usually pond water and leaf mould.'

William grinned. 'It's Brother Martin's vegetable pottage. I brought you some bread, too.'

The hob picked up the small maslin loaf and

smellt it. 'I have heard of bread.' He licked it and took a small bite of the crust with small, pointed and very yellow teeth. 'It tastes better than the pond dredgings.'

William could not argue with that. He settled himself on the floor with his back against the table leg while the hob ate his meal. The creature seemed much better this evening. Whatever Brother Snail had put in the caudle, it had worked quickly and very well. The danger with open wounds was that fever could set in and burn its way through the whole body, and sometimes turn the blood foul.

William had seen it for himself when Piers, the blacksmith in his home village of Iwele, had been kicked on the back by an ox he was shoeing. That wound had turned red and then black, and the smith had died in a fevered agony, his skin covered in black blotches.

William stirred restlessly; he tried not to think of Iwele these days. It did not help to remember the places and people he had grown up with, and though Iwele was only a day and a half's walk from Crowfield, it might as well have been a hundred days away, because he would probably never see it again. Not unless his brother, Hugh, came to take him home.

And that was not likely to happen, not when Hugh had gone off to London make his fortune three years ago and did not even know about the fire that had destroyed the mill and killed all but one of his family.

William had no idea where London was, but he knew it was far away, a mighty town full of crowded streets and people from distant lands, with a great river that led to the sea. He could not even begin to imagine what the sea looked like: water stretching away for days and weeks in all directions, with waves that could swallow a whole ship. If Hugh was there, in London, then why would he ever want to return to Iwele? No, William had long since faced the very real possibility that his brother was not going to come looking for him. He was on his own.

The hob picked out a piece of carrot from the pottage and bit into it. 'Why did you save me from the trap?'

William was startled by the question. 'I couldn't leave you there, you would have died.' He did not add, *or whoever set the trap would have killed you*, but the look in the hob's eyes told him the creature had already guessed that much for himself. People did not set traps only to rescue the animal, or hob, they caught.

'Hunting for food is one thing,' William added, 'a quick, clean kill, but maiming an animal and causing it a slow and painful death is another.'

'I have seen men commit acts of terrible cruelty, not just to birds and animals, but to other men,' the hob said, dangling a bit of leek from his fingers. 'And to trees.'

'Trees?' William frowned, puzzled. How could you be cruel to a tree?

The hob stared at him for a moment. 'They are alive too.'

'I know, but . . .'

'You have never seen a tree spirit?'

'No,' William said. 'Have you?'

The hob sucked the leek from his fingertips and fixed William with a hard stare. 'Of course.'

I suppose I should not be surprised, William thought. *If hobs exist, then why not tree spirits??*

Or angels?

William shifted restlessly. This was all so strange. A whole world existed alongside the everyday one that he had never once suspected was there.

Brother Walter was watching him closely. 'It disturbs you, knowing it isn't just *your* world, doesn't it?'

51

'Perhaps,' William said, feeling more uncomfortable by the minute, as if he had been caught out in some wrongdoing, without fully knowing what it was he was supposed to have done. 'It's just . . .'

'You didn't realise you were sharing it?' the hob suggested, eyes narrowed.

William nodded.

'Most humans don't. They believe it is theirs alone, and that all the living things in it are there for them to use as they please.'

'I'm sorry,' William said, shrugging helplessly, not knowing what else he could say.

The hob's hard green stare softened a little. 'You are not the worst human I have ever come across.'

'Thank you,' William said with a brief smile.

The hob turned his attention back to the pottage and for a while William was content to sit and watch him.

It was peaceful in the shadowy little hut, and a good deal warmer than the cold stone rooms of the abbey. William would never understand why anyone chose to build in stone. He thought of the wooden mill house, where he had grown up, and the way the timbers creaked and moved when the water wheel turned. Dust and flour from the millstones caught in the cobwebs that hung from the rafters. They waved gently, like grey rags, in the draughts coming up through the building from the millrace. The house had felt alive, somehow, with moods and a character all of its own. The abbey buildings were as cold and stiff as a corpse.

'The snail brother is a skilled healer,' the hob said, putting the empty pot on the floor and wiping his mouth with the back of his paw. 'He is a strange shape, though.'

'The bones in his back have curved forward and grown together,' William explained. 'I don't know why.'

'He can't heal himself?' the hob asked, head on one side, eyes full of curiosity.

'It doesn't seem so,' William said with a shrug.

The hob was quiet for a while, then asked, 'What is your name?'

'William Paynel. You can call me Will.' It was what he had always been called at home.

'Will,' the hob repeated. 'Will. Not Brother Will?'

William smiled. 'No. I'm not a monk.'

'Why are you here, then, living in this strange stone place with the brother men?'

'Because I have nowhere else to go. My home

53

burned down the summer before last and my family died in the fire. The monks agreed to take me in, and in return I work for them.'

The hob winced as he shifted position, trying to get comfortable. 'The brother men are kind.'

William frowned. Taking him in was not kindness on their part. It was merely recognising cheap labour when they saw it.

After the fire, the village priest at Iwele had brought William to the abbey and asked Prior Ardo to give him a home. 'He's a strong lad, and used to honest hard work,' the priest had said, turning William around for the prior to inspect, as if he was a pig at market. 'All it will cost you is his bed and board.'

'Is there nobody in Iwele who can give him work and a place to live?' the prior had asked, surprised by the request.

The priest had looked uncomfortable and asked to speak to the prior in private. William knew what he was saying, though: the boy escaped from the burning mill house without so much as a blister, while the rest of his family died. And people being what they are, they could not help but view the boy with super-stitious fear. Nobody came forward to offer him a home. Not that anyone believed he *started* the fire, of course, but it was unnatural the way he had survived it unscathed. And it was odd that he had no memory of how he had managed to get out of the burning building. One minute he was in the grain loft, the next he was standing in the middle of the yard, with no idea how he had come to be there. It set the boy apart somehow, and people were wary of him now. Too wary to want to live under the same roof as him, it seemed.

So Prior Ardo had allowed William to stay at the abbey. He had made sure William worked hard every single day to repay the abbey's great generosity. He was given a straw pallet on the kitchen floor to sleep on, and cast-off clothing several sizes too big when he outgrew his own clothes. If kindness played any part in the prior's dealings with him, William had not seen much evidence of it.

'Brother Snail is kind, and he's to be trusted,' William said at last. It was the best he could say for Crowfield and its monks.

The hob nodded in agreement, and then settled down in the basket again. 'I'll sleep now. Thank you for the food.'

William smiled as he got to his feet. He added some more wood to the fire, then picked up the hob's empty pot and the lantern. 'I'll look in on you later.'

There was no reply. The hob was already asleep. As quietly as he could, William left the hut and set off along the path through the vegetable garden. Something white suddenly loomed out of the darkness and swooped towards him. William felt a stir of air as it brushed past his face and he quickly ducked out of the way. His heart hammered with fright as he turned to stare after it. His first thought was that it was an owl, quartering the East Field and abbey gardens. The white bird landed on the roof of Brother Snail's hut. Its body hunched forward and it gave a harsh *kaa-aak*. It was not an owl, William realised in surprise, but a crow. A white crow, flying at night when others of its kind were safely roosting.

William stood on the path, watching the crow with a growing sense of unease. It was too dark to see the bird clearly but he had the distinct feeling that it was watching him. The crow's head dipped as it gave another harsh *kraak*, and then it lifted from the roof and flapped away across the river, to disappear into the woods on the far bank.

Chapter Seven

Brother Martin was in the kitchen, taking the pottage bowls from a shelf and banging them down onto the table. He glared at William.

'Finally decided to turn up, did ye? Take the maslin through to the frater, boy, and be bloody quick about it.'

William cut up the larger loaves of bread and piled the pieces into baskets, keeping a wary eye on Brother Martin as he did so. The monk slopped the pottage into a large serving bowl and carried it through the door to the frater. William followed a moment later, breadbaskets piled on top of each other in an unsteady stack.

A long table and several benches stood at one end of the large and otherwise empty room. All but two of the abbey's inhabitants were gathered into this chilly corner, sitting quietly at the table to wait for their dinner. As usual, Abbot Simon was not present. He was too sick to leave his bed and took his meals in his chamber, not that he ate much any more. And there was no sign of Peter Borowe. Lay brothers did not eat with monks, even if there were only eleven monks and one lay brother. Peter had eaten a meal of bread and cheese earlier and would have supper with William in the kitchen after the monks had been fed and the bowls washed and dried.

It was Brother Stephen's turn to stand in the wooden pulpit high up on the end wall of the room, reading from a book of prayer. He was a small, quiet man who tended the abbey's animals. He had taught William how to milk a cow, and help a ewe give birth to her lamb and the best places to look for hens' eggs, and William liked him. The monk was patient and did not waste words on unnecessary matters.

Brother Stephen would eat his meal later with Brother Martin, a prospect few of the monks looked forward to when their turn to read during dinner came around. Watching Brother Martin eat was a challenge to the strongest stomach. He fed quickly and noisily, dribbling or spitting bits of food over the table, himself and whoever was unfortunate enough to be sitting with him.

Brother Martin ladled the pottage into the bowls while William fetched jugs of small beer from the cellarium beside the kitchen and set out the mugs. To his great relief, the loaf he had taken for Brother Walter had not been missed.

It was bitterly cold in the frater. Blade-sharp draughts found their way past the ill-fitting window shutters and a vicious chill struck up from the stone-paved floor, in spite of the covering of straw and rushes.

Brother Stephen's voice was barely audible as he mumbled his way through the reading. The pulpit was reached by a spiral of narrow wooden steps and looked down over the frater, which was more than Brother Stephen could do. William could just see the round tonsure on the top of his head behind the lectern and the tips of his fingers gripping the edge of the pulpit.

The monks shivered and their cold-numbed fingers fumbled with the coarse maslin bread as they tried to break bits off to drop in the pottage. It was a cheerless meal. Prior Ardo's face was pale and drawn. He stared straight ahead, seemingly lost in thoughts that gave him no comfort. William remembered Edgar the carpenter and his strange talk of the dead angel. That must be why the prior looked as if he was carrying the weight of the world on his bony shoulders.

William caught Brother Snail's eye for a moment. The monk smiled slightly and pulled a wry face. William saw that the monk was shivering and felt a stab of concern for him. This bitter cold could not be doing him any good. William had noticed that Brother Snail's joints had been giving him more trouble than usual, and that the caudles the monk mixed for himself did not seem to ease the pain.

When dinner was finished and the monks had filed into the church to give thanks for the food, William cleared the table and wiped it down. He folded the rough linen napkins and returned them to the cupboard near the door, and then carried the bowls and mugs back to the kitchen and washed them in a pail of warm water. He had almost finished when Peter Borowe came into the kitchen and stood by the fire to warm his hands.

'Did you ask Brother Snail for the wax candle for the guest chamber?' William asked.

Peter shook his head and a look of alarm crossed his face. William smiled reassuringly at him.

'Don't worry, I'll do it later. When are the guests arriving?'

Peter thought for a moment, his brow furrowing

with the effort. 'On St Clement's day, or soon after.'

That was in two days' time.

'Do you know who they are? Or why they're coming here?' William asked. Peter probably knew more about what was happening in the abbey than anybody else. The monks barely noticed him and spoke freely in front of him. William had discovered that if you asked the right question, Peter generally had the answer.

'A Master Jacobus Bone and his manservant,' he said. 'Sir Robert of Weforde sent word to Prior Ardo at Martinmas to ask if Master Bone could come and stay here.'

William cut up bread and cheese for their supper while he thought about this. He remembered the day Sir Robert's messenger had come to the abbey to speak to the prior, because he had been told to see to the man's horse, though until now he had no idea what business had been discussed that day. Sir Robert's ancestor, Ranulf de Tovei, had been Crowfield's original patron. He had given the first monks the land to build the abbey on, and a generous gift of money, so Prior Ardo could hardly refuse Sir Robert's request.

'But *why* does this Master Bone want to come

here?' William asked, puzzled. 'Surely Weforde Manor can offer more in the way of comfort and good food? Why doesn't Master Bone just stay there?'

Peter shrugged and pulled a face. 'I don't know, Will.'

William ladled the last of the pottage into two bowls and put them on the table with the bread and cheese. He and Peter pulled up stools and sat down to eat.

'Master Bone has been Sir Robert's guest at Weforde these past three weeks,' Peter went on. 'I heard Prior Ardo say he wishes Master Bone would stay there, but he also said the abbey needs the money Master Bone has promised in return for his bed and board.'

William turned his attention to his supper. No doubt Master Bone had his reasons for wanting to come here, but William could not begin to imagine what they might be.

After supper, Peter went off to his bed in the lay brothers' dormitory, which in reality was just a small chamber that had once been a storeroom, next door to the cellarium. Years ago, when there had been more lay brothers at Crowfield, their dormitory had occupied the long first-floor room that was now the

Abbot's chamber. Peter had a bed and a chair and a tiny slit of window overlooking the yard and the pigpen. It was not much but to William it seemed like the wealth of kings.

William unrolled his mattress and blankets and laid them on the floor near the hearth in the kitchen. The *couvre-feu* guarding the glowing embers of the fire held in the heat, so the kitchen was cold. With a sigh, he lay down and pulled the blankets up to his ears. He should have been in his own bed, at home in Iwele mill, listening to the mumble of water in the millrace. Instead he was huddled up and shivering on the floor of an abbey, a kitchen boy with no home or family or future.

The world did not make much sense sometimes, William thought sleepily. There was Master Bone, paying good money to come and live at Crowfield, when William, if he'd had any money, would have paid to leave it.

Chapter Eight

Shortly after noon the following day, a cart rumbled up to the abbey gatehouse. Brother Stephen hurried out from the byre to see who was there.

William was passing a few idle moments by the pigpen, scratching the ears of Mary Magdalene, the abbey's elderly sow. Brother Stephen had managed to resist all attempts by his fellow monks over the years to turn the pig into joints of meat and boiled puddings. Instead, he bought two piglets from Weforde market every spring, to be fattened up and then slaughtered in the autumn. Prior Ardo only tolerated Mary Magdalene's continued survival because Brother Stephen made sure she did not eat too many of the scraps needed to fatten up the other pigs.

William turned to watch as Brother Stephen

opened the gate, and the cart, pulled by two horses, rumbled into the yard.

'I were towd to bring this lot here,' the carter called out. 'Sir Robert of Weforde towd me hisself, this lot to go to Crowfield. For Master Bone. He's stayin' at the manor and will follow along tomorrow, so Sir Robert says.'

'Take the cart over there,' Brother Stephen said, pointing to the west range and the outer door of the guest chambers. He turned to William. 'Go and fetch the door key, boy. Fetch both, cloister and yard. Quickly now.'

William nodded and ran off to find Prior Ardo and his hoop of keys. He found him in the cloister, looking out across the empty herb garden. His thin face was folded into tired lines of dejection and there was a faraway look in his eyes. William stood beside him for a few moments, but the prior did not seem to notice him.

'A cart has just arrived,' William said loudly, 'bringing Master Bone's possessions.'

The prior blinked a couple of times, then glanced down at William with a frown. 'No need to shout, boy, I'm not deaf.'

William reddened. 'Brother Stephen sent me to

fetch the keys to the guest chambers,' he mumbled.

The prior's frown deepened. 'And there's no need to whisper either.' He took two keys from the iron hoop hanging from his belt and handed them to William. 'Make sure you give them back to me when you're finished with them.'

The prior turned and walked away, his black habit flapping around his bony ankles and the soles of his boots rasping on the stone paving. He bowed his head to pass under the archway leading to the stairs up to the abbot's rooms.

William knew from Brother Snail that Abbot Simon was edging closer to death by the day. William had watched him mix ever-stronger potions to try and ease the abbot's pain, but the monk admitted he could do nothing to help the dying man now. It was no wonder Prior Ardo looked more grim-faced than usual.

William unlocked the cloister door of the guest chamber and hurried across to the yard door. It took a few moments to turn the large iron key in the lock, but at last he managed it and lifted the latch. Brother Stephen and the carter were waiting in the yard, stamping their feet on the icy cobbles and rubbing their hands together to try and warm them.

'Gi's a hand with the unloading, boy,' the carter said. He glanced at the monk. 'Tha's all right, in't it?'

Brother Stephen nodded. 'Very well, but be as quick as you can. The boy has enough work of his own to do.' He left them to it and went back to the byre.

William helped the carter to take Master Bone's possessions from the back of the cart and carry them through to the guest chambers.

Amongst the boxes, chests and rolled-up wall hangings, there were four musical instruments, each one inside a leather or cloth bag. There was a lute, a recorder and two flutes, one of silver and one of finely carved dark red wood.

William took the lute from its bag and gazed at it in wonder. He had seen the shawms, lutes and hurdy-gurdys of the village mummers and waits in Iwele, but they were plain and ordinary next to this wonderful instrument. The golden grain of the wood glowed in the light coming through the open doorway. It was the most beautiful thing he had ever seen.

He plucked the strings, one at a time. The pure sound shivered on the cold air and made the hairs on the back of his neck stand on end. In that moment, he knew he wanted, more than anything he had ever wanted in his whole life, to be able to make music. He wanted to play a lute like this one.

William sighed and returned the instrument to its bag. That was never going to happen. He was an orphan without a penny to his name. Lutes and the music they made were not part of *his* world.

Carefully, William laid the lute on the table, out of harm's way. He hurried out to the yard to help the carter to drag the posts and frame of a huge bedstead down from the back of the cart, and carry them indoors.

The bed was decorated with carvings of fantastic animals, the like of which William had never even imagined before. He traced the outline of a horse with a single horn growing from the middle of its forehead, and he smiled. How strange! And below it was a winged creature with a long tail and curved claws, its body twisting around one of the posts. Peering closer, William realised there were flames coming from the creature's open mouth.

'Stop idling, boy, and take t'other end of this 'fore me back breaks,' the carter called.

William looked around and saw the carter struggling with a huge oak chest, which was balanced on the edge of the cart and in danger of sliding forward and crushing him. William hurried over to help, and between them they lowered it onto the cobbles.

'Ee, that were a bugger,' the carter gasped, wiping the sweat from his face with his sleeve. He sat on the chest for a few moments to catch his breath.

'Don' s'pose there'd be any chance of some beer and summat to eat?' the carter asked hopefully.

'Ask him,' William said, nodding towards Brother Martin, who had just emerged from the kitchen and was standing in the yard nearby, watching them, hands on hips, lips drawn back in a snarl and a distinctly unfriendly glitter in his single eye.

'Mebbe later,' the carter said hurriedly. He got to his feet and grabbed a basket from the cart.

William eyed Brother Martin warily. The monk pointed at him and yelled, 'You slackin' again, soldier? I'll have ye strung up by the heels and skinned . . .'

'I told him to help the carter,' Brother Stephen called, walking across the yard towards them, wiping his hands on a wisp of straw. Fresh manure steamed on the pile beside the byre, and bits of straw and manure clung to the monk's boots. 'Peter can help with the vegetables today.'

Brother Martin did not take his eyes off William, but he did not argue. Cursing under his breath, he turned and stumped back into the kitchen.

'Master Bone certainly has a great many possessions,' Brother Stephen said in mild surprise as he looked through the doorway. 'Are those musical instruments in those bags?'

'Yes,' William said with a smile.

The monk frowned. 'Prior Ardo won't tolerate music being played for *pleasure*.' He managed to make the last word sound like a cardinal sin.

William turned away and his mouth hardened into a straight line. It was one more thing he did not understand about the monks, this dislike of music other than their own sung masses and psalms. It was as if the sight and sound of people dancing and singing for the sheer joy of it was offensive to God. He thought of Master Bone's lute and wondered how anyone, be it monk, man or God himself, could possibly be offended by any sound that wonderful instrument might make.

'But I am sure Master Bone will respect the sanctity of the abbey while he is with us,' the monk added, 'and keep his silence.'

Brother Stephen set off in the direction of the goat-pen. William watched him go and felt a flicker of anger. He hoped Master Bone would play his lute whenever he chose and send its golden notes dancing through the dark and silent rooms of the abbey.

In the largest chest, there were coverlets of velvet in dark blue and crimson. William opened another chest and found sheets of fine linen.

'Master Bone must be very rich indeed,' William said, picking up a goose-down pillow and holding it against his face. Sleeping on bedding like this would be like floating on a cloud.

The carter merely grunted. He did not seem in the least bit impressed by the finery around him.

There were other boxes and baskets tied up with rope, whose contents William could only guess at.

How could one man own so much? And why did some people have goose-down pillows and lutes, while others had nothing apart from their name and the clothes on their back?

By mid-afternoon, the cart was unloaded and Master Bone's bed pieced together. The carter did not waste his breath asking Brother Martin for something to eat and drink before he set off back to Weforde. He merely commented to William, as he glanced at the kitchen door, 'Miserable bugger, ain't he?'

William locked up the guest chamber and went to look for Prior Ardo, to return the keys. As he searched the abbey for the prior, all he could think of was the lute. He remembered something his brother Hugh had said, just before he had gone to London: 'If you want something badly enough, Will, you'll find a way to get it. Might take a while, but you shouldn't stop trying, not until your last breath.' Hugh had been talking about making his fortune in a distant town, but his words applied just as well to William's new-found desire to make music.

William found the prior standing by the foot of the stairs to the abbot's quarters, talking to Brother Gabriel. He caught the last snatch of their conversation before they noticed him.

'. . . we can't afford to turn him away,' the prior said.

'But what shall we do when the others find out?' Brother Gabriel said, sounding flustered.

'We will worry about that when the time comes, which we must hope will be after he has paid the abbey the money he promised . . .' The prior saw William and broke off. He glared at the boy. 'What do you want?'

William held out the keys. 'We've unloaded Master Bone's possessions and I've locked up.'

The prior took the keys. 'Go about your work, and don't let me catch you listening into conversations that do not concern you again, or you will be punished.'

'I wasn't!' William said, stung by the unfairness of his words.

'Do *not* argue with me, boy!'

William scowled and walked away. He turned down the passageway beside the chapter house and set off across the garden. By the time he reached Brother Snail's workshop, his anger had faded and he had begun to wonder what it was the prior and Brother Gabriel were trying to hide from the other monks.

The hob was sitting by the fire, poking the embers with a stick and humming softly to himself. There was a small pile of hazelnuts on a hearthstone, their shells blackened from being roasted in the fire. He carefully chose four and held them out to William. 'I saved these for you.'

'Thank you,' William said, touched by this generosity. Hazelnuts were the hob's favourite food. He sat on the floor and cracked the shells with his teeth.

'Where did you get these?' William asked, hoping they weren't from the abbey store room.

'I found them.'

'Where?'

'They were hidden in the hollow tree near the bend in the river. By a squirrel.' There was a gleeful expression on his small face. 'A *hungry* squirrel.'

73

For a few minutes, they sat in companionable silence, eating the hazelnuts and gazing into the fire. William's thoughts turned to Master Bone's lute. *One day, people will sit and listen to me play an instrument like that*, he thought with a deep certainty. *They'll nod and agree that they've never heard anything so wonderful before. I don't know how, or when, but I will make it happen somehow.*

Chapter Nine

St Clement's Day was wrapped in a shroud of fog. The abbey, a cheerless place at the best of times, was gloomier and chillier than usual. The fire in the kitchen burned sullenly that morning and seemed reluctant to part with any heat. William riddled the embers and broke up a couple of branches to add to it. He crouched beside the hearth and watched as small flames licked the new wood.

There was a tight knot of excitement in his stomach. Master Bone was due to arrive some time that day. William thought of the musical instruments, waiting for their owner in the guest chambers, and he smiled gleefully. Perhaps now the endless silence of the abbey would be broken occasionally, and he might finally hear the golden lute being played.

William's first task of the day, after seeing to the fire, was to fetch water from the well in the yard and take it to the kitchen and the monks' lavatorium in the west cloister alley, where they washed their hands and faces before going through to the frater to eat. After that he would take a pail to Brother Snail's workshop. Today, there would be one extra trip to the well, to fetch water for the guest chambers.

By the time the monks filed into the chapter house for the daily meeting, William had delivered water to the lavatorium and the guest chambers and had hung a cauldron of water to heat over the kitchen fire. He carried a pail of water up the day stairs to the reredorter beside monks' dormitory, where he washed the wooden seats of the latrines. He poured the last of the water away, down into the drain that ran below the row of small wooden stalls and out into the river. A small stream had long ago been diverted to run through the drain, to flush it out, but even so, Peter still had the all-too-frequent job of cleaning out the drain itself. William would sooner be thrown out of the abbey and left to starve than crawl through that fetid stone tunnel, clearing away the build-up of human waste. He and Peter had to make do with the small wattle-walled latrine hut on the far side of the yard. Peter had to clear out the cess-pit beneath that, too.

William set off to take a pail of water to the work-shop. The fog drifted like a mournful ghost through the trees on the edge of the abbey vegetable garden. Beyond the trees, the world faded to nothing. The cawing of the crows, high up in the branches of Two Penny Copse, sounded far-off and eerie.

In the monk's graveyard, beyond the wattle garden fence, Peter Borowe stood, a dark shape in the fog, staring at the ground. Even from this distance, William could see the unhappy droop of Peter's shoulders. He set the pail down on the path and walked over to see what the lay brother was doing.

Peter stood beside the shallow beginnings of a grave, shovel in hand. He looked at William but said nothing. There was no wave or smile today. William could see the trail of tears on Peter's mud-streaked cheeks. His thick brown hair was lank from the damp fog.

William looked down into the dark scrape at his feet. 'Whose grave is this?' he asked.

'It's for Abbot Simon.'

William stared at him in shock. Abbot Simon was dead? Shouldn't the passing bell be ringing? 'When did he die?'

Peter shook his head. 'He's still alive. Prior Ardo

thought it would be wise to dig the grave before the ground freezes again, just to be ready.'

'Why isn't he being buried in the chapter house?' William asked, puzzled. It was where all Crowfield's abbots were buried. William had glimpsed the stones marking the graves through the doorway, carved with crosses and letters and set amongst the red and white floor tiles.

Peter shook his head again. 'Abbot Simon wanted to be out here, in the sunlight and air, not laid beneath cold stone in the darkness.'

William opened his mouth to say that the abbot would hardly be in the light wherever he ended up, and that it surely wouldn't matter much one way or the other, but thought better of it. Peter was upset enough without William adding to it.

The sight of the pile of brown earth on the ground beside the grave gave William a tight feeling in his chest. For a few moments he was back in the church-yard in Iwele, standing beside the four heaps of newly dug earth that covered the graves of his family. He had been too numb to feel anything that day. It was only later, when life in the village had moved on and returned to normal, that the pain started. It washed over him now in a wave of raw grief, catching him off guard. He quickly blinked away the tears that blurred his eyes.

He would not feel anything when the abbot died because he had never really known him, but Peter would. Abbot Simon had taken Peter in when he was a child and had shown him great kindness and patience, by all accounts. William felt sorry for the lay brother, but there was nothing he could do to lessen his pain. It was something everyone had to face sooner or later.

'Will,' Peter said suddenly, nodding to something behind William, 'look.' William glanced around and saw a large white crow standing on the path a few paces away. One blue-grey eye watched him intently. He was sure it was the same bird he had seen here the other evening. It showed no fear and made no attempt to move off the path. William waved a hand at it, in the hope it would hop or fly away, but it did not move.

Peter squatted down and whistled softly to the crow. The bird's sharp gaze flicked from William to the lay brother. Peter whistled again. He looked up at William with a puzzled frown.

'He wants you to follow him.'

'It told you so, did it?' William asked, grinning.

Peter nodded. 'You have to go with him *now*.'

William looked down into Peter's face for a few moments and realised he was being entirely serious. 'I didn't hear it say anything.'

'I didn't hear him in words,' Peter said. He tapped the side of his head. 'It is just a kind of knowing in here.'

The crow waited patiently. Its head was turned so one eye stared unblinkingly up at William.

'Where does it want to take me?' William asked, a vague feeling of unease beginning to creep over him.

Peter stood up and shrugged. 'I don't know, Will. He didn't tell me that.'

William took a step towards the crow. The bird moved a little way along the path with an odd little hoppity-skip and then stopped again. It continued to watch William beadily, a fierce expression in its eyes. William picked up the pail of water for the workshop and followed the crow cautiously along the path. The crow stayed a few steps ahead, hopping and walking by turns, and disappeared around the corner of the hut.

William paused by the rainwater barrel. The bird's strange behaviour made him feel uneasy and he wondered what waited for him behind the hut. He glanced back at Peter. The lay brother was still standing by the partially dug grave, watching him anxiously. Taking a deep breath, William walked around the corner.

The crow stood on the bench outside the hut door, where Brother Snail sometimes sat on warm days in the dappled shade of the blackthorn tree. A few paces away stood a woman. He was sure he knew most of the villagers from Weforde and Yagleah, by sight at least, but he had never seen her before.

The hem of her green woollen cloak was damp and muddy, as were her scuffed leather boots, and she leant heavily on a hazel stick. She was small and neat of build. Her hair was hidden under a linen hood tied beneath her chin, and her weather-browned face was finely webbed with wrinkles. But it was her eyes that held William's attention. One eye was pale milky blue and the other one was light brown, unsettling eyes that stared at him as if seeing beneath his skin. The crow leant forward and gave a harsh caw.

The woman's head turned towards the crow. 'Keep watch, Fionn. Warn me if any of the holy brothers approach the hut.' She said the words 'holy brothers' contemptuously. The bird rose into the air with a rustling flap of its glossy white wings and glided away over the hut roof.

'You shouldn't be here,' William said, setting the

pail down. If Prior Ardo caught her, there would be trouble. Women were not tolerated in the abbey precinct; they were permitted into the nave of the church to hear mass, though none had ever come to Crowfield while William had been living there. To see one here in the garden was a little shocking.

'I have more right here than you do.' Her voice was as harsh as her bird's. She swung the stick around the foggy garden and orchard. 'And more right than any of those crow-robed men of God will ever do.'

William stared at her as if she was mad. How could the woman have more right to be at Crowfield than the monks did? That made no sense. She did not *look* mad, but that did not mean she wasn't. 'What do you mean?'

Her strange eyes narrowed to slits and the lines on her face seemed to deepen. 'You will find out for yourself one of these days.'

That sounded like a threat, William thought, taking a cautious step backwards. There was something about the old woman he did not like, a subtle air of menace that was out of keeping with her appearance.

'What's your name, boy? Are you a novice here?'

William shook his head. 'No. I'm a servant. And my name is William Paynel, of Iwele.'

She was silent for some moments. Her thin hands, the nails black and the parchment-dry skin ingrained with dirt, folded around the top of the stick. 'Tell me this, how does a boy like you come to have the gift of Sight?'

'The Sight?' he repeated, startled. 'I don't.'

'No? Yet you found an injured hob in Foxwist Wood and brought it here. Such creatures are rarely seen by humans, but *you* saw it.'

William stared at her warily. His first instinct was to deny all knowledge of the hob, but he shrugged that aside. He had the feeling it would not be wise to lie to her.

'I found the hob in a trap in the wood,' William said slowly. 'His leg was hurt. I freed him, and he has been staying at the abbey while he heals.'

'You brought it here to the crippled monk,' the woman said, nodding. 'He has the Sight too, it would seem. He's not like the others who live here. I've seen him gathering plants in the woods and the fields. He's a good man.'

The woman seemed to know a great deal about what had been going on these last few days, William realised. She knew all about Brother Snail too.

'I want see the hob for myself, to make sure it is

being tended to properly,' the woman continued briskly, pointing to the hut with a curved claw of a finger.

'Brother Snail has done his best for him,' William said, nettled by this.

'I am sure he has, but he has never treated a hob before.'

'And you have?'

'On occasion,' the woman said mildly, ignoring his rudeness. 'Now, perhaps you will let me into the hut?'

William hesitated. What would she do if he refused? And why hadn't she merely let herself in? Was there some reason why she could not go inside Brother Snail's workshop uninvited?

'I will ask only once,' she said softly, her eyes glittering.

A cold shiver went down William's back. He walked to the door and lifted the latch, fervently hoping he was not making a mistake in letting her into the hut. Without a word, she brushed past him and stepped over the threshold. William followed close behind.

The hob was curled up in the empty wood basket. The firewood was piled neatly on the floor nearby. He was fast asleep and snoring softly in little wheezy whistles. His tail hung over the side, and bits of straw were stuck in the tuft of reddish hair at the end.

The woman stood just inside the doorway. The slightest of smiles pleated the wrinkles at the corners of her mouth as she looked down at the sleeping hob. She glanced at William and nodded as if satisfied. 'I can see that it is in good hands. You have done well, you and the monk.'

There was a rustle of wings as the white crow landed on the path outside the hut door. It gave one hoarse *Kaa-ak* and hopped up on to the bench. The woman turned towards the bird with a frown. 'Fionn warns me that someone is coming this way.' She looked back at William. 'If you ever need my help, go to Weforde and ask for me there. Tell them you are looking for Dame Alys and they will tell you where to find me.'

She pulled up the hood of her cloak and left the hut. William followed her out and closed the door behind him. He stood for a few moments to watch her weave her way amongst the apple trees in the orchard. The white crow, Fionn, flew after her, soaring over the treetops and disappearing into the fog.

Footsteps scrunched on the gravel path leading to the hut. William went to see who was coming, and to his dismay saw that it was Prior Ardo. His cowl was pulled up and his face was hidden in shadow, but it was unmistakably him. He walked quickly, his hands tucked into the wide sleeves of his habit, and for a moment, panic rattled through William. What if the prior went into the hut and saw the hob?

The prior looked up at William and frowned. 'What are you doing here, boy?'

'Bringing water to the workshop for Brother Snail.'

The prior pushed back his cowl. 'I saw someone making off through the orchard. Who was it?'

William thought quickly. 'A villager from Weforde, begging for some vegetables from the garden.'

'Begging?' the prior snapped. 'Stealing, more like. Did you give him anything?'

'No.' At least that much was true. William was relieved to realise the prior did not suspect that the unwelcome beggar was a woman.

'And was that a white bird I saw on the roof of the hut?' The prior's voice was heavy with suspicion. 'A crow, perhaps?'

William shrugged and pulled a face. 'I don't know.'

The prior's eyes narrowed. 'If you see a white crow on abbey lands, boy, tell me immediately. Is that clear?'

William nodded.

'The bird is an abomination and must not be tolerated to live,' the prior added, his thin fingers touching the heavy iron cross hanging on a leather cord around his neck.

William stared at the monk's thin, humourless face with dislike. Was he prepared to kill a bird merely because its feathers were the wrong colour? Or was there some other reason he hated the crow?

'Don't idle there, boy. Go about your work.' The prior turned on his heel and set off back along the path towards the abbey.

William let out a sigh of relief. That was far too close a shave. He and Brother Snail would have to take more care to keep the hob hidden. If the prior wanted to kill the crow for the sin of being white, then what would he do to the hob?

William sat on the bench beside the hut door for a few moments, thinking about Dame Alys. Did he really have the Sight, as she seemed to believe? And Brother Snail too?

William knew all about the Sight; Old Mabby, back home in Iwele, had the Sight. She was a mad old crone who had a ramshackle hovel full of animals and birds that she had tamed and cared for over the years. If anyone had a wart to charm away, or needed a love potion, or something darker, they went to Old Mabby. The villagers treated her with a fearful respect but her gift set her apart from them. Being different was rarely a good thing to be. William didn't want the Sight and he definitely did not want to be different.

But want it or not, he knew he had no choice in the matter. Dame Alys had called it a gift, but that remained to be seen. It could just as easily be a curse.

Chapter Ten

The foggy afternoon had darkened into a blind dusk when two horsemen rode along the track from Weforde and crossed the bridge to the abbey gates. Prior Ardo had ordered a lantern to be hung on a post beside the bridge and a second one in an upper window of the gatehouse, to guide the travellers to the abbey. William, instructed by the prior to watch for their arrival, ran to open the gate as soon as he heard the hollow ring of hooves on the bridge and the jingle of harness.

The horsemen waited silently while William dragged the heavy gate wide enough to allow them to ride on into the yard.

Burning with curiosity, William stared at the abbey's guests. The first one through the gate was a man with long silver-white hair, tied back with a strip of leather. The lantern light picked out a web of scars on his pale face. He was slim of build and not particularly tall, as far as William could judge. It was impossible to guess his age. He might have been twenty years old, but he might just as easily have been forty. There was something timeless about the thin, sharp-boned face that William found unsettling.

The man glanced down at William as he rode past. There was no friendliness in his expression. 'Tell your prior that my master, Jacobus Bone, has arrived,' he said, his voice as soft and cold as a snowdrift.

William looked at the second man and felt a shiver of unease. Master Bone wore a black cloak with the hood pulled up. His shoulders were hunched and he sat stiffly in the saddle, looking like a scarecrow propped up on the horse's back. But what disturbed William the most was that he was wearing a mask. It was a brown leather mockery of a face with two holes cut out for the eyes and a fold of leather poking out like a beak over a hole for the nose.

The horsemen rode on across the yard and disappeared into the fog. William closed and barred the gate and ran after them.

The scar-faced man was helping his master to dismount. Moving slowly and awkwardly and gasping with pain, Master Bone leant heavily on his servant as he half-slid, half-fell from his saddle.

William watched them for a moment, then sprinted through the kitchen and collided with Brother Gabriel in the cloister alley.

'Ouf!' the monk grunted, grabbing William's shoulder to steady himself. 'Walk, boy, before you do someone a mischief,' he snapped.

'Master Bone and his servant have arrived,' William said quickly. 'They're in the yard by the kitchen door.'

'Fetch the prior. He's with Abbot Simon. I'll go and greet our guests.' The monk hurried away.

William ran along the dark cloister to the stairs up to the abbot's chamber. It was as black as a moonless night through the archway. He could hear the murmur of voices coming from upstairs: prayers for the dying, as the abbot's life slowly ebbed away.

Taking a deep breath, William set off up the narrow stone steps. He reached the landing at the top and knocked softly on the door. The praying continued. He knocked again, a little louder, and heard a shuffling sound in the room beyond. The door opened a crack and Brother Snail's face appeared.

'William,' he said, sounding surprised. 'What is it?'

'Master Bone is here.'

Brother Snail nodded and turned to speak to

someone in the room behind him. A moment later, the door opened wide and Prior Ardo stood there. William caught a glimpse of the abbot's room. A fire burned on the hearth and shadows flickered across the lime-washed walls. A large wax candle stood in an ornate silver holder at the foot of the bed, where Abbot Simon lay propped up on pillows. His skin was a sickly yellow and hung loose on his bones, and his eyes had sunk back into their sockets. His lips were ringed with blue and his breathing was a harsh rasp above the monotonous flow of prayers from the two monks kneeling by the bed. William stepped back, repelled by the cloying smells of sickness, sweat and incense.

'Where are they?' the prior asked briskly, nodding for William to go ahead of him down the stairs.

'In the yard with Brother Gabriel.'

The prior handed William the two keys. 'Unlock the doors and light the candles. I will go through the kitchen and meet them in the yard. Be quick, boy.'

A fire had been burning in the guest chamber fire-place all day but it had barely taken the chill off the room. William unlocked the yard door and left it ajar while he lit the rushlights in their brackets around the walls.

The yard door opened and Prior Ardo ushered Jacobus Bone into the room.

'We are a small house and not used to guests,' the prior said, frowning around the draughty chamber. He stared at the two men for a few moments as if trying to decide what to make of them. 'Firewood and water will be brought to you each morning, and your meals will be served in here. If there is anything else you need, Brother Gabriel will see to it.'

Master Bone inclined his head in a slow nod of acknowledgement. 'Thank you for the water and firewood,' he said, his voice little more than a hoarse whisper, 'but my servant, Shadlok, will prepare my food.'

Prior Ardo looked a little startled. 'As you wish. We can give you flour and vegetables, and carp from the fishponds . . .'

'That will not be necessary,' the man interrupted. He sounded weary and the strength seemed to leave his body. Shadlok stepped forward and took his arm. He guided his master to the chair beside the fire.

'My servant will provide whatever food we need.'

'Very well, if that is what you would prefer,' the prior said, glancing at Brother Gabriel and raising his eyebrows. William could almost hear his thoughts.

What food could he possibly hope to scavenge around Crowfield in the winter? There was little enough to feed the monks as it was.

'Master Bone needs to rest after the journey,' Shadlok said. He stared at the prior until the monk took the hint.

'We will leave you to get settled,' Prior Ardo said stiffly. 'The boy will see to your horses.'

The monks left the room and William walked over to the yard door.

'Wait, boy,' Master Bone said, without turning in his chair. He sat awkwardly, his body bowed forward. His breathing sounded laboured.

William paused with his hand on the door latch.

'Come closer, into the light.'

William walked back to stand in front of Master Bone. The man's eyes glittered through the holes in the mask, and seemed to be the only thing about him that was fully alive.

'What is your name?'

'William Paynel.'

'How old are you?'

'Fourteen years, last Easter.'

'Are you an oblate?'

William shook his head. Oblates were children

94

given to religious houses, to be brought up in the ways of the abbey or nunnery. Thankfully he had been spared *that* fate. 'I was orphaned and taken in by the abbey. I'm a servant.'

He shifted uncomfortably from one foot to the other. The heat from the fire warmed his leg, a painfully pleasant feeling. He wanted to turn and hold his hands out to the flames, to feel the aching chill leave his bones.

'Did your family live in Weforde?' Master Bone continued.

William frowned, wondering where all this was leading. 'We lived in Iwele. My father was the miller.' He paused. Master Bone seemed to be waiting for more. 'The mill burned down over a year ago.'

'Is Iwele near the abbey?'

William shrugged. 'A day and a half's walk away.'

'Do you ever leave the abbey? Perhaps to go into the woods hereabouts?'

What a strange question, William thought. 'I often go to the Wednesday market in Weforde with Brother Gabriel, and I collect firewood and take the abbey pigs to forage in Foxwist Wood.'

William glanced at Shadlok, who was standing behind his master's chair. He was watching William with a disturbing intensity. The firelight lit his face and William saw him clearly for the first time. The scars on his cheeks and neck were old, just thin white lines against his pale skin. They looked like slashes from a blade. The man's eyes, deep-set above sharply jutting cheekbones, were ice-blue. There was something about them that made William shiver. An unsettling thought slid into his mind: they were the eyes of a wild animal, not a man.

William looked away, but he could still feel Shadlok's cold, unblinking stare. It was as if he could see inside William's head and was picking through his thoughts and memories.

William edged away from the fireside. 'I have to see to the horses,' he said, glancing at the yard door, anxious to be away from the guest chamber and its strange occupants.

'Very well. We will talk again.' Jacobus Bone lifted a hand in dismissal. The cuff of his long sleeve slipped back just far enough to reveal part of his hand. Or what was left of it. William stared at the stumps of two fingers and a thumb and caught his breath in shock.

Jacobus Bone was a leper. That was why he wore the mask, to hide what the disease had done to his face.

William met Master Bone's steady gaze and felt the blood burn up into his cheeks. His first impulse was to turn and run from the room. Hot waves of horror washed over him as he remembered how he had handled Master Bone's possessions, his bedding and the golden lute. He had touched everything that leprous body had touched. He shuddered and took a step back from the man in the chair.

The thought of the lute was like a thump in the middle of William's chest. He would never hear it being played now.

William turned and walked quickly to the door. He glanced back once before he left the room. Master Bone and Shadlok were still watching him, silent and unmoving. It was a relief to close the door behind him and set off across the yard, to lead the horses to the stables.

Why had Prior Ardo allowed a leper to live alongside his monks? It seemed very out of character for the usually cautious prior. Then he remembered the snatch of conversation he'd overheard between the prior and Brother Gabriel. The prior had mentioned being paid for something. Was it to let Master Bone stay at the abbey?

William lit the lantern just inside the stable door.

He led the horses into stalls and took off their bridles and saddles. He dried their damp flanks with straw, rubbing their chilled bodies to warm them. The abbey's solitary horse, Matilda, whinnied softly to the new arrivals. William fed his two charges and gave the elderly grey mare an extra couple of handfuls of oats.

When the horses were settled for the night, William stood in the stable doorway and stared uneasily out into the darkness. He had the oddest feeling that there were things moving through the fog, slipping silently and unseen across the yard towards the abbey. He thought he could feel the passing of fleet-footed bodies, disturbing the damp air so that it swirled through the light from the lantern and brushed William's face like deathly cold fingers.

Alarmed, he quickly stepped back into the stable and closed the door. Nothing would persuade him to leave the stable until he was sure that they had gone, whoever or whatever they were.

Shivering as much from fear as cold, William huddled in a corner of Matilda's stall, glad of the mare's warm and solid presence. She whickered softly and nuzzled his hair with her lips. William smiled and reached up to stroke her soft nose.

The abbey no longer felt like a safe place to be.

Shadows seemed to be gathering around its cold stone walls, a darkness that went beyond the presence of a leper and his pale-eyed manservant. Strange things were afoot. William knew he would have to keep his wits about him in the coming days.

Chapter Eleven

illiam was woken from a bad dream shortly before dawn by the *clang-clang* of the bell for lauds. He had slept badly and was bleary-eyed with tiredness as he rolled up his mattress and carried it through to the storeroom beside the kitchen. He riddled the embers on the hearth and added branches to get the fire going. Pulling up his hood, he hurried across the yard to fetch water.

The fog had lifted during the night, and the morning was grey and damp and very hard on the spirits. William yawned and stretched sleep-stiffened muscles as he stood for a few minutes by the well. Light showed around the edges of the shutters covering the windows of the guest quarters. He thought of Jacobus Bone, sitting in the chair by the fire or lying in the carved bed beneath velvet coverlets, and a shiver went through him. The thought of having to take water and firewood to the guest quarters every day filled him with dread.

As soon as the monks were at mass, William took two apples and a small piece of cheese from the store-room beside the kitchen. He wrapped them in a napkin, with a piece of bread left over from the previous day's baking. The crust was as hard as stone but it was still reasonably soft inside. He tucked the bundle of food inside his tunic and set off for the workshop.

The hob was standing on a stool beside the table. He was grinding something in the stone mortar with a pestle. His face was puckered into a frown of concentration and he took no notice when William came into the hut.

'What are you doing?' William asked, peering into the mortar.

The hob glanced up at William. 'That is a stupid question.'

'I mean,' William said, 'what's *that*?' He nodded to the green, pungent-smelling paste in the bottom of the stone bowl.

'Wolf's-bane root. The snail brother tries to hide it, but his bones ache. This will help him.'

The hob's knowledge of plants rivalled that of the monk. Indeed, Brother Snail had confided in William that he had learned a great deal from Brother Walter over the last few days and would be sorry to see him leave. Not that the hob seemed in a hurry to go anywhere, William noticed. He had made himself quite at home in the hut, and could get around surprisingly well with the help of the crutch William had made from a forked ash branch. He was healing quickly and had expressed an interest in seeing the rest of the abbey, much to William's alarm.

William took the napkin of food from his tunic and put it on the table. The hob put the pestle down and inspected the contents of the napkin. 'No hazelnuts?'

'Sorry, no. There is a small basket of nuts in the storeroom, but Brother Martin will know if I've taken any and he won't be happy.'

'The brother with the slow wits, he was digging a grave hole yesterday,' the hob said, picking up a small green glazed pot and pouring a few drops of almond oil into the ground-up roots in the mortar. 'Who is it for?'

'Abbot Simon. He's dying. The prior thought it would be a good idea to dig the grave while the ground is soft, before the frosts return.'

'You bury all your dead together in fields of graves,' the hob said, his small leathery face wrinkling thoughtfully as he looked up at William, 'but you do not do it for other creatures. Why is that?'

William squatted down by the fire and warmed his hands. Why did Brother Walter have to ask so many difficult questions?

'I suppose,' he began slowly, thinking about it, 'we don't bury pigs and sheep, birds, cattle and fish because they're food. They're not the same as people,' he finished with a shrug.

The hob turned to look down at William, the golden-green eyes widening in astonishment. 'They are just the same in here,' he said, patting his chest.

'They don't talk or think like us,' William said. 'They have no souls.'

The hob wiped his paws on a rag and climbed awkwardly down off the stool. He tucked the fork of the crutch under his arm and limped over to the hearth to stand in front of William. 'I can talk, and I have a spirit that will never die, but I am not human.'

William was feeling more uncomfortable by the minute. 'But you're . . . different. Not animal, not human.'

'So would you bury me in your field of graves with

the brother men if I died today?' he asked.

'Eh, no, probably not,' William muttered, feeling himself redden.

'Why not? Because I am not as important as the brother men? I do not *matter*, perhaps?'

'You aren't a Christian creature,' William said. 'You can't be buried in a churchyard if you are not Christian.'

'Why?'

'Because only Christian souls go to heaven.' That was what the priest at Iwele had told him, so it must be true, William thought, though he was no longer quite so certain of that. The hob's questions were forcing him to look harder at things he had accepted without a second thought before.

'So where do you think all the other spirits go?' The hob lowered himself onto the floor and eased his injured leg into a comfortable position.

'I don't know,' William said. It was one more thing he had never thought about.

The hob shook his head. 'You know so little, human. One day, I will take you to the woods and show you where they go.'

William did not like the sound of this. 'They're all in the woods?'

The hob glared at him and made an impatient sound. 'Tcha!'

Which told William nothing. He had a disturbing vision of huge herds of ghostly animals roaming through Foxwist, all the creatures hunted and slaughtered for food over the years, though he had never seen as much as a ghostly whisker there before. Perhaps the hob had magical powers and could make him see things he normally missed.

The hob turned his attention to picking bits of straw and dried leaves from his fur. 'Maybe that is why the brother men buried the winged creature in the wood. They did not want its spirit near their abbey.'

William frowned at him. 'What winged creature?' As he said it, he remembered what he had overheard by the abbey gate: an angel, dead and buried. His heart began to beat a little faster. '*What* winged creature?'

'It was shot with an arrow and it died in the snow out in the woods, one midwinter, many years ago. I do not know what manner of creature it was.'

'What did it look like?' William asked. Surely it could not really have been an angel?

'I did not see it, but I heard it was as high as this hut.' The hob pointed to the roof rafters. 'It had skin the colour of shadows on snow, and feathered wings from its shoulders to its feet.'

'It was an angel,' William said softly, a shiver going down his spine.

'A nangel?' the hob said with a questioning frown.

'They live in heaven with God,' William explained. 'They serve Him.'

The hob was quiet for a while. His ears twitched like a cat's as he puzzled this over. Something was clearly troubling him. 'If they live with your god, then they must be very important.'

William nodded. 'Very.'

There was an odd look in the hob's eyes as he stared at William. 'So why did the brother men hide the nangel's body in the woods? Why did they not bring it here to the grave field? Won't your god be very displeased that they treated his servant like that?'

William could think of nothing to say to this. The hob was right, though. Why had the monks buried it so quickly and in secret? Surely finding an angel, alive or dead, would be a thing of great wonder? A miracle, even?

'How do you come to know about the angel?' William asked.

'I heard about it from a hob who used to live in the

woods. He was being hunted by a fay king and the nangel came to his aid. The king killed the creature with his bow, and the hob escaped. He never knew what manner of creature had helped him. If I see him again, I will tell him it was a nangel.'

William stared at Brother Walter uneasily. It seemed the woods were more crowded than Weforde on market day.

'Comnath, the Dark King of the Unseelie Court, is an ancient and powerful fay warrior,' Brother Walter said softly, his voice tinged with fear. 'He has not been seen in these parts since he killed the nangel. He is evil and dangerous and will hunt down any creature unlucky enough to catch his eye.' The hob shuddered and drew a little closer to the fire. 'Those who live in the woods are fearful that he will return one day soon. Whispers have reached us that he was seen not far from here at midsummer. I do not know if it is true but I hope it is not.'

'What will happen if he does return?'

'All the solitary fays will be given a choice: join the king's court or be hunted to death. It is hard to know which would be worse.'

'Is that what you are?' William asked curiously. 'A solitary fay?'

The hob nodded. 'And I want to stay that way.'

'Even if it means being hunted by the Dark King?'

The hob hunched his shoulders and stared unhappily into the fire.

'Well, you're safe in the abbey. If ever he comes after you, you can come here.'

The hob did not reply. It suddenly occurred to William that perhaps the abbey walls would not offer protection against the fay king. Perhaps he could hunt wherever he chose and nothing could stop him. After all, he had killed one of God's own angels with perfect ease. It was a terrifying thought.

William got to his feet. He had work to do, and he wanted time to think about everything he had learned that day. One thing he was sure of, though, was that he wanted to find out more about the angel. There was only one person he could safely ask, and that was Brother Snail.

'I have to go. Oh, I almost forgot.' He paused with his hand on the door latch and looked back at the hob. 'A woman with a white crow came to the hut yesterday, to make sure you were safe here at the abbey. She said her name was Dame Alys. Do you know her?'

The hob pulled himself to his feet with the help of the crutch and limped over to the stool beside the table. His small face was carefully expressionless and he did not meet William's gaze. 'I have seen her in the woods, collecting roots and berries. She is a healer, like the snail brother.'

William waited but the hob did not add anything further. He was sure the hob knew more than he was saying but he did not have time to stay and find out what that might be.

'I will bring you more food later,' William said, opening the door.

The hob nodded. 'Bread, but no more pottage.' He pretended to stick his fingers down his throat and made a gagging sound.

William grinned and left the hut.

As he walked along the path to the abbey, he wondered how it was possible that an angel could die. Surely, if they lived in heaven, they were not made of flesh and blood? How could a single arrow, fay or otherwise, kill one?

And if angels could die, then could the unthinkable happen? Could God Himself die too?

Fear knotted in William's stomach at this terrible thought. As soon as he could, he would speak to Brother Snail and just hope and pray the monk could answer his questions.

Chapter Twelve

Later that morning, Brother Martin told William to fetch a pail of water and go and scrub the long table in the frater. William had almost finished his work when Brother Snail came to clean the pewter candlesticks and replace the tallow candles. He made them in his workshop, dipping wicks of hemp into smelly vats of melted mutton fat. He had made the last batch with William's help and it had taken a great deal of determined scrubbing with wood ash and cold water for William to get the pungent smell of sheep grease from his hands.

Brother Snail glanced at William. 'You seem pre-occupied today, Will. Is there anything wrong?'

William straightened up and took a deep breath. 'I know about the angel.'

The monk seemed to turn to stone. His smile faded

and he stared at William with a look of shock on his face.

'How did you find out about it?'

'I overheard Edgar from Yagleah talking to the prior. And the hob knows all about it, too.'

'I see.' Brother Snail lowered himself slowly and stiffly onto a bench and stared at the floor for a while in silence.

'And I know monks from the abbey buried the angel in the woods,' William added, watching him warily. Should he have kept what he had found out to himself?

'The angel has been a closely guarded secret for nearly a hundred years,' Brother Snail said at last, his face pale and his eyes troubled. 'It is Crowfield's curse. What did the hob tell you about it?'

William sat down beside the monk. 'He said the angel was killed by a fay king one midwinter night. The angel was trying to save a hob from the king, so the king killed him instead.'

Brother Snail's eyes were wide and bright as he listened intently to this. 'A fay king?'

William nodded. 'Brother Walter called him the Dark King of the Unseelie Court.'

'We never knew who fired the arrow, or why, until

now,' the monk said softly. He held out his arm. 'Help me up, Will.'

William took his arm. The monk leant heavily on him as he got to his feet.

'Since you already know so much, I have something to show you. Come with me.'

William followed the monk out into the cloister alley, and around to the door of the sacristy, a small room beside the chapter house where the abbey's books and few valuable possessions were kept locked away. Brother Snail took a ring of keys from the small purse hanging from the cord around his waist. With a quick glance around to make sure they were not being watched, he selected one and unlocked the door. He ushered William inside and lit the candle in the lantern hanging from an iron bracket on the wall.

'Close the door, Will.'

The monk unlocked a wall cupboard in a corner of the room. Candlelight gleamed on silver and William glimpsed a chalice and two candlesticks.

Snail took a plain oak casket from the cupboard and laid it on the small table in the middle of the room. He hesitated for a moment, and then lifted the lid. Inside was a folded piece of faded blue silk.

William held his breath as Brother Snail carefully

lifted the silk aside to reveal what William thought for a moment was a long silver blade. It gleamed with a soft moon-white sheen in the candlelight. Then William realised it was not a blade, but a single white feather.

'One of the monks who buried the angel found this in the snow. It has been kept here, safe and secret, ever since.' Brother Snail's voice was barely more than a whisper. William thought he saw the gleam of tears in the monk's eyes.

'Brother Walter said the angel was buried in the woods,' William said. 'Why wasn't it brought here and buried in the graveyard or in the abbey church?'

'The abbot couldn't allow that, Will. Nobody could know about the angel, don't you see?'

William shook his head, puzzled.

'If people found out that an angel could die like some mortal creature of clay, it would raise doubts about the nature of angels, and perhaps even God Himself, and they would ask questions for which we have no answers. It would shake the church to its very foundations. As far as the world outside these gates is concerned, angels cannot die. It is Crowfield's curse that we have to know and guard the terrible truth.'

'Then how come Edgar of Yagleah knows about it?' William asked.

Brother Snail gazed down at the feather. 'It was a Yagleah man who found the dying angel that night. It was Christmas Eve in the year 1243, and he was returning home after visiting friends in Weforde. He ran to the abbey for help but the angel had died by the time the abbot and two of his monks reached it. The villager helped the monks to bury the body, and the abbot swore him to secrecy.' Snail was quiet for a moment. 'Perhaps the burden of such a secret was too much for the man. He told his son, and over the years, the secret has been passed down from father to son, all the way down to Edgar. When the stranger came to Yagleah asking questions about an angel, only Edgar knew what he was talking about.'

'So how did the stranger find out?'

The monk frowned. He folded the silk over the feather again and closed the box. 'I don't know, Will.'

'Whereabouts in the woods is the angel buried?' William asked as Brother Snail returned the box to the cupboard.

'Nobody knows, not even Edgar. Whatever else was passed down through his family, it didn't include that.'

'Where was the body found?'

'On the track to Yagleah, near the ford over the Sheep Brook.'

William knew the place. The track from Weforde crossed the brook at the foot of Gremanhil. Huge old oak trees grew on the lower slopes of the hill. The Sheep Brook ran deep and shadowy through the trees before curving out into the sunlight and along the edge of the abbey's East Field.

Snail opened the door and waited for William to go ahead of him, back out into the cloister. 'Say nothing of this to anyone.'

William shook his head. 'I won't.'

They walked back to the frater. As they passed the door of the guest chamber, William said, 'Did you know that Master Bone is a leper?'

The monk stopped and twisted his head around to stare up at William in astonishment. 'Are you sure?'

William nodded. 'I saw his hand, or what's left of it.' He curled his fingers over his palm in a pale imitation of Master Bone's ruined hand. 'And he wears a mask to hide his face.'

Brother Snail looked worried. 'I didn't realise that he did. I haven't seen our guest yet. Are you sure his hand wasn't injured in an accident, Will? Maybe a fire?' A flush of colour rose into the monk's face as he realised what he had said. 'William, I'm sorry. I didn't think . . . it was tactless of me.'

William looked away. He knew what a fire could do to a person. He had seen the remains of his parents and his sister and brother after they had been dragged from the smouldering wreckage of the mill.

'He's a leper,' William said softly.

'Then in God's name, why has the prior allowed him to come here?' Snail said with a rare flash of anger. 'I must speak to him straight away. Go about your work, Will.'

William was startled by the monk's tone and his abrupt dismissal but did as he was told. He was in a thoughtful mood as he went back to the frater to finish scrubbing the table. Perhaps Brother Snail could make the prior see reason and persuade him to send Master Bone away. He had heard that some of the larger abbeys had leper hospitals, well away from villages and towns. Master Bone could find shelter in one of those.

William dried his hands on the front of his tunic and carried the pail of water back through the kitchen, to empty it in the yard.

Brother Martin was skinning a rook. Several more, some already skinned, some just stiff little corpses of glossy black feathers, were lined up on the table beside him. He was taking the skin and feathers off in one piece, saving himself the bother of plucking the birds. He glanced at William when he came into the kitchen.

'Make yerself useful and fetch some herbs from Brother Snail's workshop,' he growled, chopping off the rook's head with one slash of his knife. It joined a small pile of heads on the blood-stained table. He slit the raw pink body open and hooked a finger into the cavity to drag out the innards. William stared in horrified fascination.

'Fetch somethin' *strong*. Garlic, mebbe,' the monk said, scraping the rook's innards into a pile and wrinkling his nose at the smell that rose from them. 'Somethin' *really* strong.'

Something to mask the taste of stewed rook. William was not sure anything would be able to do that, no matter how pungent.

William left the kitchen and headed across the yard towards the gate between the far corner of the south range and the goat- and pigpens. It was the long way around to the workshop, but William wanted to be by himself for a while, out of the chilly gloom of the abbey buildings. After all the talk of the angel and the fay king, he wanted to be somewhere as everyday and ordinary as the abbey garden.

The grey day clung damply to the abbey buildings and softened the mud in the yard. The crows high up in the treetops of Two Penny Copse were subdued that morning. As well they might be, William thought grimly, after seeing what had happened to the rooks. Brother Martin was surprisingly good with a sling-shot, given that he only had one eye. The crows were probably anxious to draw as little attention to themselves as possible.

William caught a movement out of the corner of his eye, over towards the pigpens. Something small and reddish-brown moved past a gap in the wattle fence. Frowning, William went to see what it was.

The hob was sitting on the edge of Mary Magdalene's water trough, his injured leg stretched out along the rim. A new growth of fur bristled around the healing wound. His tail was curled up his back and over his shoulder to keep it out of the water. The pig sat in front of him.

'What are you doing here?' William hissed, glancing quickly around the yard. 'You should be in Brother Snail's hut, not out here in the open. Someone might see you.'

The pig turned at the sound of William's voice and shuffled over to him, grunting softly, in the hope of some food. William scratched her ear.

'I wanted to see the abbey,' the hob said with a dismissive wave of his paw. Then he nodded towards Mary Magdalene. 'The pig sees all the comings and goings from her pen. She has seen some strange things these last few days.'

'She told you that, I suppose?' William said, raising his eyebrows.

The hob nodded and tapped his forehead. 'We can talk in here. Not in words.'

Just like Peter and the white crow, William thought, looking down into the pig's intelligent amber eyes. She gazed back at him calmly and he knew, without doubt, that the hob was telling the truth.

'What has she seen?' he asked.

'Two strangers came to the abbey yesterday,' the hob began.

William nodded. 'Jacobus Bone and his servant. They are staying here.'

'And behind them, there were two others, creeping through the fog. The pig could not see who or what they were.'

'I sensed that there was something in the yard last night, though I couldn't see anything either,' William said, a shiver going through him at the memory. It had been a long time before he had dared to run back to the safety of the kitchen. He had locked the door and sat huddled by the kitchen fire late into the night, wondering what was lurking in the foggy darkness outside. It had not made for a good night's sleep.

The hob gazed at him thoughtfully for a moment, head on one side. 'You are unusually sensitive to such things, for a human. You have the Sight.'

'That's what Dame Alys said.'

Again, that odd shuttered look came into the hob's eyes. William was more certain than ever that the hob knew something about Dame Alys that he was in no hurry to share. He knew the hob well enough by now to know he would be wasting his time trying to prise it out of him.

'It seems that someone is very interested in Jacobus Bone and his servant,' William said. 'I wonder why?'

The hob shrugged. 'Who knows?'

'He's just an old man who, I think, has come to Crowfield to die,' William added quietly. 'He's a leper.'

The hob sat upright in a quick jerky movement that startled William. He grabbed the edge of the trough with both paws to stop himself falling backwards into the water. 'A leper?'

William nodded, astonished by the sudden widening of the green-gold eyes and the fierce expression on the hob's face.

'Has he brought anything with him, an instrument of any kind? A lute, perhaps?'

'Yes, along with two flutes and a recorder. Why?' William asked, his heart beginning to beat a little more quickly.

'Is it a lute made of golden wood?'

'Yes,' William said, his breath catching in his throat. 'How did you know?'

The hob ignored his question. 'Bone's manservant, what is his name?' he said the last word softly.

'Shadlok.'

'Ahhh,' the hob breathed out in a long juddering sigh. He banged the sides of his head with his fists. 'Sceath-hlakk. Shadlok. Of course! Of *course*!' He turned and glared at William. 'If you had said his name straight away, we would not have wasted all this time in idle talk.'

'You know him?' William asked, too surprised by the hob's alarming behaviour to be offended.

'No, but I know *of* him, and of the one you call Bone. And I know who is following them. This is not good, Will Paynel, not good at all.'

Chapter Thirteen

'Sceath-hlakk is a fay of the Seelie Court,' the hob said, talking quickly. 'A great warrior.' He waved his skinny little arms in wide arcs to emphasise just how great a warrior Shadlok was. 'He was once the consort of Yarael, a queen of the Seelie Court and age-old enemy of the Dark King. I think the Dark King knows they are here, and the creatures in the yard last night were his Unseelie fays.'

William could easily believe the scar-faced man was a warrior. There was something in his bearing, a cold arrogance that made William think he would be a formidable opponent. And he could readily believe Shadlok was not human; it was there in his eyes.

'What is the difference between Seelie and Unseelie fays?' William asked.

'The Seelie Court fays are the Blessed Ones, good for the most part,' the hob explained. 'The Unseelie are the darkness to their light.'

'Why is Shadlok here? And why is he the servant of a leper?'

'I do not know,' the hob said, shaking his head and looking worried. 'Sceath-hlakk was exiled from Queen Yarael's court hundreds of winters ago. Nobody knows why. The one you call Bone was the queen's minstrel, the most gifted musician ever to have played for a fay queen.'

'Is he a fay as well?' William asked, trying to make sense of this strange story.

'Bone is human,' the hob said, climbing the wattle fence awkwardly, wrapping his tail around a post to steady himself.

William glanced around to make sure nobody was watching, then picked up the hob and put him on the ground.

'But he cannot die,' the hob finished. He limped over to the gate. William noticed that he no longer needed to use the crutch. It seemed fays healed much faster than people did.

William pushed the gate open and let the hob go through ahead of him.

'The queen gave Bone the gift of music, and for a time he was famed in every court and nobleman's hall in countries far and wide,' the hob continued, as he set off along the path towards the orchard. 'The Dark King decided to punish the queen for giving such a gift to a human. A terrible and bloody war between the two courts was waged. Neither side lost, but neither won, so the king took his revenge on Bone in the cruellest way he could think of. He made Bone a leper, and then made him immortal. Bone is cursed to wander the world for all eternity,' the hob finished softly.

'That's *horrible*.' William thought of Jacobus Bone's hand and was filled with pity. What a terrible punishment for simply being the best at what he did. 'But if Master Bone isn't here to die, why *is* he here?'

The hob shrugged. 'Perhaps this is just the next step on an endless journey.'

'No,' William said thoughtfully, 'he came here for a reason. He paid the prior to be allowed to stay. He could have gone anywhere, but he chose to come here.'

'I can think of nothing that would bring him here,' the hob said, looking up at William. He pulled a face and added, 'I can think of no reason *anyone* would want to come here.'

William smiled. 'You did.'

'It was either that or die in the woods.'

'You'll soon be well enough to go back to Foxwist,' William said. He realised he would miss the hob when he was gone.

'I will stay here for now,' the hob said. 'If the Dark King's fays *are* following Bone and the Seelie fay, then the woods are no place for a solitary fay to be.'

'I'm not sure you'll be much safer here,' William said, 'if the Dark King's fays can come and go so easily inside the abbey walls, though they will be the least of your worries if Brother Martin or one of the other monks sees you. You should go back to Brother Snail's workshop and stay out of sight.'

The hob nodded. 'The pig will keep watch on the yard for us, but we must find out why Bone is here.' He looked at William through narrowed eyes. 'And you can tell the brother man with the slingshot to stop killing the rooks.'

William smiled thinly. 'You can't tell Brother Martin anything. The rooks will just have to take their chances.'

'They will not forget what he has done,' the hob said darkly.

If it came to a fight between the monk and the rooks, William knew whose side he would be on.

William and the hob made their way along the path through the orchard to Brother Snail's workshop. The hob let himself into the hut while William went to see what he could find in the small herb garden. Brother Snail grew pot herbs here and his medicinal plants in the herb garden in the cloister. Most of the plants had died back over the winter. Only a woody old sage bush and some straggling thyme had managed to survive the cold weather. Brother Snail had long since cut and dried last summer's herbs and hung them in bunches from the workshop rafters. The roots of most of the plants were deep in the earth, waiting for the first warm days of spring to shoot again.

William broke off a handful of sage stems and sniffed their pungent scent. He would need something with a stronger flavour than sage to hide the taste of rook meat. Not that there was anything growing at Crowfield, or anywhere else, that was going to make this evening's supper edible, and even for Brother Martin, that was quite some achievement. With a sigh, he tucked the sage into the pocket of his jacket and went to see what he could find in the hut.

When word got out that one of the abbey's guests was a leper, the monks were horrified. William heard angry voices when he passed the door of the chapter house with a basket of firewood for the warming room. He paused to listen for a few moments.

'You condemn us all!' someone shouted. It sounded like Brother Stephen, normally the mildest of men. 'This is a most ill-judged action . . .'

'Master Bone has been generous,' Prior Ardo said, a hard edge to his voice. 'Crowfield Abbey is a poor house, we all know that. We cannot afford to turn away a wealthy benefactor, leper or not.'

'What use will his money be when we are all eaten away by this sickness?' Brother Odo called, his voice shrill with fear. 'Most of us have our health and strength but we barely survive from one year to the next as it is. What hope will we have when we lose our hands, our feet? All the money in the land won't help us then.'

'Master Bone's money will buy two cows next spring, as well as an extra pig, and will pay for repairs to the nave roof. These are things we *need*,' Prior Ardo said.

'I *need* my fingers,' Brother Mark said. Brother Snail had told William that Mark was a gifted illuminator and scribe. From time to time, he was commissioned to produce a psalter or a book of hours for some wealthy nobleman. This was a welcome source of income for the abbey. William knew it was only this money, and the rents from the tenants of Crowfield's two farms near Yagleah, that kept the monks from destitution.

The monks all began to talk at once, shouting each other down and drowning out the prior's attempts to regain control of the meeting.

William left them to it. He took the wood to the warming room and built up the fire. It was a small, windowless chamber, one of the few rooms in the abbey to have a fireplace and chimney. The monks were permitted to come in here for a short time on cold days, and warm their chilblained hands and feet. If the wind was in the wrong quarter, though, smoke would blow back down the chimney and fill the room. In wet weather, the fire would spit and sizzle or burn with sullen reluctance. But there were no fires in the frater or dormitory, and the church seemed to hold the cold within its walls even in high summer, so those precious minutes in the warming room were a much-valued privilege, smoke or no smoke.

William stacked the logs and branches on the floor near the fireplace. He pulled up a stool and sat for a few moments, hands out to the small flames.

Today, there was no wind. The logs on the hearth burned cheerfully. William took off his scuffed old boots and held his feet out to the flames, sighing with pleasure as the feeling returned to his chilled toes.

What would Prior Ardo and the monks do if they knew the truth about Jacobus Bone? What would they say if they found out that Shadlok was not even human? William smiled briefly. What uproar that would cause.

With a sigh, William pulled on his boots and stood up. He put the fire screen across the fireplace and went back out into the draughty cloister. The monks were still in the chapter house but they were talking now, not shouting.

William turned the corner into the south cloister alley. His heart seemed to stop when a figure stepped out of the shadows near the stairs up to the abbot's lodgings. It was Shadlok, his hair and skin startlingly white against his dark clothing. The unsettling blue eyes held no hint of friendliness.

'Master Bone wishes to talk to you,' he said. Without waiting for William's reply, he turned and walked away, his boots making no sound on the stone-paved floor.

William hesitated. The last thing he wanted to do

129

was go anywhere near Jacobus Bone, but he had the feeling that it would be unwise to cross Shadlok.

William paused in the doorway to the guest quarters. The windows were shuttered and the only light in the room came from the small fire burning in the hearth. There was no sign of Shadlok and all he could see of Jacobus Bone was the top of his head above the back of the chair beside the fire.

'Come in, boy.' Jacobus Bone's voice was little more than a whisper but it echoed in the stillness of the chamber.

William walked slowly across the room, keeping as far from the man in the chair as he could. He jumped when the door closed with a hollow bang behind him. He turned quickly to find Shadlok, arms folded, standing by the door, watching him. His face was expressionless and his cold eyes reflected the firelight. William swallowed a couple of times, but his mouth and throat had gone dry.

'Over here, where I can see you,' Jacobus said. He was sitting stiffly in the chair, just as he had been the previous evening. Had he been there all night?

He had removed his hood. The mask was still in place, and above it William could see his hairless, ulcerated scalp. His ears were just lumps of discoloured flesh. If he was aware of William's revulsion, he gave no sign of it.

'I want your help, boy.'

William waited for Jacobus to continue. His stomach was churning and he tried not to stare at the man's ravaged head. He was uncomfortably aware of Shadlok standing behind him, still and silent, blocking his way to the door.

'The monks are not pleased to have a leper living amongst them,' Jacobus said. 'Even now they are asking their prior to send me away, so I may not have much time at Crowfield Abbey.'

It seemed William had not been the only one eavesdropping that morning. He stared into the dark eyes and wondered if this was what Jacobus Bone's life was like: always shunned and turned away, even by monks who prided themselves on their charity towards those in need.

'Will you help me, boy?'

William hesitated. 'Help you with what?'

Jacobus shifted in his chair. He rested his elbows on the carved arms and leant forward. 'I have come here to find something. You know the woods and fields around the abbey. Perhaps you can help me to find it.'

William glanced over his shoulder at Shadlok. Whatever these two were up to, some instinct told him he would be foolish to get involved. 'What is it?'

Jacobus nodded, once, slowly. Without a word, Shadlok crossed the room and lifted the lid of a chest. He took out a roll of vellum tied with a narrow red silk ribbon and handed it to William.

'Look at it,' Jacobus said.

The vellum was a piece of fine and smooth calf-skin, unlike the rougher and far less expensive sheep-skin parchment used by the Crowfield monks. William unrolled it and saw that it was a page cut from a book, a book of hours, perhaps. The text was decorated with small coloured pictures. William had seen Brother Mark working on pages such as this at his desk in the cloister, before they were gathered together and bound into books.

'Look closely at the drawings,' Jacobus said. 'Tell me what you see.'

William angled the page to catch the light from the fire. The words were meaningless to him, just black lines and curves crawling across the page like neat rows of ants. Along the right-hand margin of the page were two long-bodied dragons, one blue, the other red, biting each other's entwined tails. There was a

132

single, large letter in a blue and gold square in the middle of the writing. Behind it was a man in red robes with the lower part of his body in the jaws of a large fish: Jonah, perhaps, being swallowed by the whale. William knew the story from the priest at Iwele, who liked to liven up his sermons with spirited retellings of Bible stories. William peered closely at the drawing and smiled briefly at the look of surprise on Jonah's face.

'There are dragons, and Jonah and the whale,' William went on, glancing up at Jacobus. He looked back at the page and tried to make out the details in the three small drawings at the foot of the page. They were enclosed by a border of crows amongst twisting branches and leaves.

The first picture showed a hill with trees growing on the top, and in the foreground a white-robed figure with feathered wings. There was what appeared to be the shaft of an arrow sticking out of its chest. A chill went through William as it dawned on him what he was looking at.

The second picture showed a group of black-robed figures carrying a shrouded body. Their tiny faces looked anxiously out of the page, as if frightened of discovery. Behind them, the dark-blue sky was dotted with gold stars and a full moon. In front of the huddle of monks was an acorn, which struck William as odd. The acorn was the same height as the figures and carefully painted, as if the artist had wanted to make sure it looked as realistic as possible.

The third picture was harder to make out. William moved closer to the fire so more light fell on the page. What at first just seemed like a jumble of shapes resolved themselves into a white feather and something that looked like a hazelnut.

'Well? What else do you see?' Jacobus asked softly.

'I . . . I'm not sure,' William muttered.

'Then look closer.' Master Bone's voice was as soft as thistledown, but it held an edge of suppressed excitement that William did not like.

'I think . . .' he began, and then hesitated. 'I think there is an angel. And monks. And a feather. And an acorn.'

Jacobus nodded. 'Very good, William. Now tell me, does any of that mean anything to you?'

'Why would it?' William's voice sounded odd to his own ears, too high and strained. He could not look Jacobus in the eyes.

'The hill with the trees, do you know of a place like that hereabouts? And look at the picture again. What of the animal behind the angel?'

Animal? William frowned and looked again. Yes, now that he was looking for it, he could see something small and white, almost hidden by a fold of the angel's robe.

A sheep, he thought suddenly. Didn't Brother Snail say the angel died at the ford over Sheep Brook? Was the sheep a clue to the name of the place? And if the first picture showed Sheep Brook ford, then the hill behind it was Gremanhil.

He peered at the other two drawings with renewed interest. Perhaps the acorn and the hazelnut, and the crows in the border, were also clues to place names? The crows could mean Crowfield.

William met Jacobus's steady stare. Should he tell him what he knew? He decided against it, for now. He would keep it to himself until he found out what Jacobus Bone wanted with the angel. He shook his head and shrugged, and feigned an air of ignorance.

'The hill with the trees?' Jacobus said, with a trace of impatience. 'Do you know such a place?'

'There are hills everywhere around here,' William said. 'Crowfield is in a valley. So is Weforde, and you have to go over two hills to get to Yagleah. There are trees on most of them. Except the small one north of

Yagleah. There is a windmill on that one.'

Jacobus sat back in his chair, his movements slow and stiff. His eyes never left William's face.

'I see,' he said evenly. 'Very well, you can go.'

Shadlok appeared at William's side and held out a hand for the vellum page. William gave it to him and for a couple of moments, their eyes met.

A shiver of unease went through William. He had the feeling Shadlok knew he was hiding something. He would wager that Shadlok was the stranger who had been asking questions in the local villages about the angel.

William walked quickly to the door and stepped out into the cloister alley. He took deep breaths of damp morning air and leant against the wall for a moment, relieved to be away from the dark room and its unearthly occupants.

At least now he knew what Jacobus Bone was doing at Crowfield Abbey, even if he did not know *why* he was so interested in the angel.

But whatever his reasons, they were important enough to have brought him to Crowfield in winter, a difficult enough journey for someone young and in full health, and Master Bone was neither.

As William hurried off to the relative safety of the

kitchen, he told himself he would have to be careful. If Shadlok and Master Bone suspected he knew more about the angel than he was saying, then what were they prepared to do to make him talk?

Chapter Fourteen

The monks had finished discussing the problem of what to do about Master Bone and had filed out of the chapter house in a solemn-faced line. Brother Stephen came looking for William.

'I want you to take the pigs into Foxwist,' he said, 'to forage. Stay there until the prior sends word for you to bring them home.'

William looked at the monk in astonishment. Take the pigs to forage in *winter*? He had spent a few weeks in the woods with the pigs early in the autumn, watching over them while they foraged for beech mast and acorns in the abbey's old deer park. The Weforde villagers had rights of pannage in Sir Robert's part of Foxwist, but nobody had told the pigs where the boundary was, and they often strayed onto abbey land and helped themselves to the acorns there. It meant that by now, the ground was all but bare. Brother Stephen knew that as well as William did, but it seemed the monk was in no mood to discuss the matter.

'Well, don't just stand there, boy,' he said briskly. 'The pigs won't take themselves into the woods.'

The monk walked away. He had big feet and his boot soles slapped on the muddy cobbles like hand-claps.

William stared after him in dismay. Under different circumstances, he would have been delighted to go into Foxwist with just the pigs for company, but now it was the last thing he wanted to do. Somewhere out in the woods were fay creatures who thought nothing of killing an angel. The only good thing about leaving the safety of the abbey walls was that he would not have to eat Brother Martin's rook stew for supper.

William hurried to the kitchen and packed some bread, cheese and apples in a leather bag, enough to last a couple of days, until Peter brought more food out to the wood for him. He was rolling up his blanket when Brother Martin banged open the yard door and came into the kitchen. He stood in the doorway, hands on hips, and stared at William.

'You bin in the guest chambers today?' he growled.

William nodded. 'Master Bone asked to see me.'

The monk made a strange gurgling noise in his throat and crossed himself. He stood aside and pointed out into the yard with one meaty fist. 'Out!' he yelled. 'Get yer leprous hide out of this kitchen, and don't come back.'

'I don't have leprosy,' William said angrily, picking up the bag and cramming the blanket into it.

'Out!'

White-faced with fury, William slung the bag over his shoulder and walked to the door. He paused beside the monk and saw the fear in his eye. The monk backed away and crossed himself again. Without a word, William stepped out into the yard. The door slammed behind him.

William felt sick. Is that why he was being sent out to Foxwist? Because the monks believed he might have caught leprosy from Master Bone?

The thought made him go hot and cold in quick succession. Perhaps the monks intended to leave him in the woods and not allow him back to the abbey at all. They would not send Peter with food and he would be left to starve.

William's hands were shaking as he pulled up his hood. Surely, if they wanted him to go, they would not be sending him off with the abbey's pigs? They were worth far more than he was. The monks would never risk losing *them*.

He crossed the yard to the pigpens. Mary Magdalene was lying in the straw in her thatched shelter. The two younger pigs in the next-door pen were rootling through a pile of scraps. William knew Brother Stephen had intended to slaughter them in the next day or so. That would have to wait now, though the monk had already put it off as long as he could to make sure there would be meat, however sparse, through the winter months. William leaned over the fence and rubbed one of the pigs on its back, glad that the animals' last few days would be spent out in the woods, and not in this small muddy pen.

'William!' someone called.

William looked over his shoulder and saw Brother Snail hurrying across the yard towards him.

'I'm glad I caught you before you left,' Snail said breathlessly, one thin hand pressed to his chest. 'I tried to talk the prior out of sending you into the woods, but he wouldn't listen.'

'Does he think I might be a leper now too?' William asked, straightening up. 'Is that why he wants me to go?'

The monk's eyebrows shot up. 'Of course not, Will. Quite the opposite. He wants to keep you safe, and that means keeping you away from Master Bone. He will see to it that water and firewood are left outside the door to the guest chambers every morning, but beyond that, he doesn't want anyone from Crowfield having unnecessary contact with our guests. You can bring the pigs home as soon as Master Bone leaves the abbey.'

Relief surged through William but it was short-lived. That was one worry out of the way, but another, darker one took its place.

'It's not safe in Foxwist,' William said, folding his arms around his shivering body. He hesitated, then, looking away, added softly, 'I'm scared.'

He would not have admitted that to anyone else, but Snail understood.

'I know, Will, I know.' The monk took a small bundle from inside his sleeve and held it out to William. 'It isn't much, but it might help against . . . any unwanted visitors to the hut.'

William unwrapped the square of cloth. Inside were several iron nails, a few twigs with withered leaves and shrivelled berries, and a folded scrap of waste parchment. William opened it and found a dried clover leaf tucked inside. He looked up at the monk with an uncertain smile. 'How will these help?'

Brother Snail picked up the twig. 'This is rowan, an effective protection against fays. Keep it close to you. Wear it inside your tunic.'

'What do I do with these?' William asked, picking up one of the nails.

'Hammer them into the wood around the hut door, but keep one back. Carry it with you at all times. Fays do not like iron. It burns them if they touch it, and if they stay close to it for long, it poisons them.' The monk smiled briefly. 'Brother Walter assures me it works.'

William frowned. 'But I saw him chopping leaves with a knife the other day.'

Brother Snail took his small herb knife from his belt and held it out to William. 'The blade is made of bronze, not iron.'

'What about the clover leaf?'

'Clover usually has three leaves. This one has four. It can break a fay spell and dispel glamour, so you can see any fay in its true shape.' The monk pulled a small lead cross on a leather cord from beneath his habit and handed it to William. 'And wear this, too.'

William put the cross around his neck. He wrapped

the nails, clover and rowan twigs in the cloth and tucked them inside his tunic.

'How do you know about these things?' he asked. In his experience, monks did not believe in fays and suchlike. Brother Snail not only knew they were real, he seemed to have an understanding of their ways.

The monk smiled. 'I have not always been a monk, William. When I was a boy, I was sickly and did not play much with the other children. My father was a freeman and comfortably wealthy, so I was neither needed nor expected to work on the land. Instead my time was spent in the fields and woods, learning about the plants and the creatures that lived there. I think I have always known there was another world, a hidden, magical place existing alongside our own. I could sense it out there in the wild places, where the hand of man has not left its mark.'

'But you chose to be a monk,' William said, puzzled. He could not imagine Prior Ardo giving him advice on how to protect himself from fays. Anything with the faintest whiff of magic that crossed the prior's path was likely to be tied to a stake and burned or damned to hell for all eternity. How could Brother Snail live amongst men who saw evil in things that were merely different?

'I chose to worship God in the only way I could, Will,' Brother Snail said with a smile, 'by living quietly and simply, and helping any of His creatures, be they man, beast or fay, in need of my skills. Is that so hard to understand?'

'No,' William said after a moment's thought, 'I suppose not.'

The monk was quiet for a moment. 'The prior and men like him follow their own path to God. Perhaps theirs is just that bit longer.'

And with a few more potholes and heading in the wrong direction, William thought, but he kept that to himself.

'Oh, I nearly forgot,' Snail said, holding up a hand. 'One more thing.' He took a harness bell from the pouch hanging from his belt. 'The hob told me fays do not like the sound of bells. I think he meant church bells but this will have to do, because I'm sure Prior Ardo wouldn't be too happy to see you haul the bells down from the church tower and drag them into the woods with you.'

William shook the bell and grinned at the small jingle it made. 'I don't think this would scare a flea, let alone the Dark King, but thank you anyway.'

'Take no chances, Will.'

'Don't worry, I won't,' William said, putting the bell inside his tunic. He glanced around to make sure there was nobody about and added, 'Jacobus Bone knows about the angel.'

'He does?' Brother Snail sounded startled. 'How did he find out?'

'He has a page from a holy book with pictures showing its death and burial.' William described the details in each picture. The monk listened intently, a look of worry shadowing his eyes.

'Did he say where he found this book?'

William shook his head.

Snail lowered himself slowly and stiffly to sit on an upturned pail beside the pig pen and rested his hands on his knees. William squatted down beside him, so their faces were level.

'One of the monks who helped to bury the angel that night left soon after for the abbey of Our Lady of Bec, in France,' the monk said. 'He was a fine scribe and illuminator. He must have continued his work at the French abbey, and for some reason, he hid the story of the Crowfield angel amongst the illuminations. I am sure that is where Master Bone must have found the page.' The monk was quiet for several moments. 'But it doesn't explain why he is so keen to find out more about the angel. What did you tell him, Will?'

'Nothing.'

'Good,' Snail nodded. 'We must keep it that way until we find out what he's up to. Now,' he slapped his knees and forced a bright smile, 'it's time for you to be on your way.'

There was a sinking feeling in the pit of William's stomach as he stood up and helped the monk to his feet. In spite of the things Brother Snail had given him for protection, he felt as if he was about to climb into a bear pit.

'With luck, the prior will send Master Bone on his way in a day or so, and you'll be back home and safe before you know it.'

William opened the gate of Mary Magdalene's pen. He hoped the monk was right, because somehow, he did not think the Dark King of the Unseelie Court was going to be fended off with a withered twig and an old harness bell.

Chapter Fifteen

The bells for sext rang out from the tower of the abbey church as William and the pigs set off into Foxwist. Mary Magdalene, who had made this journey many times over the years, was content to trot along beside William. Every so often, she stopped to rootle through a pile of dead leaves or nose a patch of earth, grunting softly to herself. The two younger pigs ran off in all directions, excited by their unexpected freedom. William rounded them up if they strayed too far, prodding them back onto the trackway with the pig-stick, an ash rod dark and shiny from countless years of use by abbey swineherds.

From the moment he crossed the bridge by the abbey gatehouse, William had the feeling he was being watched. The feeling persisted when he turned off the main trackway and headed northwards. He was tense and watchful as he walked along, but whatever was keeping pace with him through the trees remained hidden.

The track skirted the abbey's hazel coppice and reached a bank topped by a wattle fence and stretches of thorn hedging. It had once enclosed the abbey's deer park, a remnant of more prosperous days, but there were no deer there now. Over the years the hedge had thinned to a straggle and the fence had fallen in places and lay rotting under the leaf litter. Now the park was only used to provide pannage for the abbey pigs, and the pigs of Crowfield's two tenant farmers.

The ditch was shallow and easily crossed. William climbed the bank, herding the pigs ahead of him. The undergrowth was sparse here. There were wide clearings around ancient oaks and stands of birch trees, and open sweeps of bracken. This was the heart of Foxwist, a place of deep green shadows in summer and mist and silence in winter. Local people told stories of strange creatures that haunted the glades on moonlit nights, of fays that danced between the trees. As William walked along, the stories came back to him and he wished that he was safely back inside the walls of the abbey.

The swineherd's hut stood on a low ridge overlooking a stream. Its wattle and timber walls leaned to one side and had been propped up with a couple of huge oak branches. The thatch was green with moss and thorny whips of bramble twisted through it. In spite of its ramshackle air, the hut was weatherproof. Firewood was stacked against one wall beneath the overhang of thatch. A small wooden pail hung from a nail by the door.

William dropped his bag on the ground and set off down to the stream to fetch water. The pigs were already there, drinking. Mary Magdalene would not stray far from the hut but he knew he would have to keep an eye on the other two. He rubbed his arms to warm himself as he stood on the stream bank and looked around. He no longer felt he was being watched but he knew he would be foolish to believe that whoever it was had gone for good. They would be back sooner or later, of that he was sure.

William carried the pail back to the hut. He pushed open the door and peered inside. It was just as he had left it the last time he had stayed here. The bed, a frame of planks piled with dried straw and bracken, stood against the end wall. William poked through the bedding with the end of the pig-stick, to make

150

sure there were no small creatures settled there for the winter, then unrolled his blankets and spread them out.

The hut was simply furnished with a stool, a small stone-lined fire pit and a lantern hanging from an iron hook on the wall. An old iron cooking pot, black with soot but scrubbed clean inside, stood on a flat stone by the fire pit, and a *couvre-feu* lay nearby.

William took the bundle Brother Snail had given him from inside his jacket and laid it on the stool. He gathered up the nails and went outside to look for something to use as a hammer. He found a stone by the stream and used it to drive the nails into the wood around the door, then tucked the last nail inside the rolled-up cuff of his jacket sleeve.

The wind had shifted around to the north and the day was growing noticeably colder. The sky between the branches of the oaks was a clear pale blue and the low winter sun threw long shadows across the clearing. It was going to be a bitterly cold night.

William looked around for somewhere to put the rowan twig, and decided he wanted to keep it close. He put it under his blanket at the head of the bed. He slipped the four-leafed clover, still inside its fold of parchment, into his other jacket cuff. He hoped it would be enough to protect him from whatever might walk the woods after dark.

William went to fetch some firewood. The pigs were nosing through a drift of oak leaves nearby, searching for acorns, grunting and throwing leaves around and generally enjoying themselves. William smiled as he stopped for a moment to watch them.

He made a small rick of branches in the fire-pit and opened the tinder box he had brought with him. He took out the little strip of steel and the flint and poked a charred scrap of linen into place over bits of dried toadstool and flax. He had done this so many times before, but he still loved the sight of sparks dancing off the steel and touching the cloth, and the tiny curl of smoke as the sparks caught and fire was born.

Carefully, William blew on the tinder to coax the small flame to grow. He set fire to the pile of dry bark kindling in the fire-pit, then quickly patted out the fire in the tinder box. He sat back with a satisfied smile as the flames grew and licked the branches. For now, he was content.

Mary Magdalene came to the hut doorway and stood watching the fire.

'You're welcome to join me,' William said, grinning at her.

As if she understood his words, the pig came into the hut and flopped down by the fire pit. William laughed and prodded her with his foot.

'Don't get too comfortable. We have to go and find the other two soon, before they take it into their heads to run away.'

Mary Magdalene closed her eyes and gave a contented grunt. For now, old age and a love of comfort won out over the lure of acorns.

The fire settled and William put the *couvre-feu* in place. The pig did not stir as he left the hut, so he closed the door quietly behind him and left her to sleep.

A chilly breeze ruffled his hair and chilled his cheeks. He pulled up his hood and blew into his cupped hands to try and warm them as he looked around for the pigs. They were foraging beneath an oak tree on the far side of the stream. William herded them back towards the hut. By the first shadow-fall of dusk, the two pigs were safely penned for the night.

William piled on the floor for Mary Magdalene what few acorns he had managed to find in the woods earlier that day, along with several small, wrinkled apples. When she had finished her meal, he led her out to the pen. She walked wearily into the shelter and settled down in the pile of bracken with her two companions.

William returned to the hut. It was warm and smelled of pig. He sat on the floor by the fire to eat his supper of bread, cheese and water. Somewhere close by, an owl hooted, a breathy hoo-*hoo-ooo* that emphasised the silence around it. William felt a small stirring of unease. The pigs had kept him busy that afternoon and he'd had little time to worry. But now, alone in the hut in the dark woods, he felt vulnerable. The hut walls did not seem like much protection against whatever might be outside.

William built up the fire. He tried to think of cheerful things: summer days in Iwele, swimming in the river with the other village children; the Michaelmas goose fair on the green; working in the mill beside his father and brother; and later, sitting by the fire listening to his mother telling stories, tales rich with magic and colour, like the best of dreams. He could remember her voice and the way her eyes almost closed when she laughed, and how she would sing sometimes, when she thought nobody could hear her. His memories were as precious as a purseful of silver pennies.

William yawned and stretched his arms. The smoky

warmth was making him sleepy. He covered the fire and lay down on the bed. He wrapped himself in one of the blankets and wriggled around to get comfortable on the pile of bracken and straw.

He was drifting on the edge of sleep, his body tired and relaxed, when he became aware of a rustling in the roof thatch. He opened his eyes and listened. The wind, maybe? The rustling became louder. Bits of straw showered down between the rafters and onto his face.

Fully awake now, William sat up, spitting straw and thatch out of his mouth. More scattered over him. It was not the wind, or a rat in the thatch. It was too big for that.

Something was trying to get into the hut.

Chapter Sixteen

William grabbed the rowan twig and clambered out of bed, banging his shin on the wooden frame. He backed away until he reached the hut door, kicking aside the *couvre-feu* as he stumbled over the fire pit. He held the twig out in front of him. It was a small dark shape against the glow of the embers in the pit. He must have been stupid to believe that a bit of dead wood could do anything to protect him against fays.

He had two choices: run into the dark wood and hide, or stay in the hut and fend off whatever it was with the rowan twig.

As choices went, William thought grimly, one was as bad as the other.

'Ouf!' Something fell onto the bed in a rush of thatch. William's heart seemed to leap out of his chest. He held the twig out in front of him like a sword, while desperately scrabbling behind him for the door latch.

'Stay back,' he said, his voice shaking. 'I warn you, this is rowan and it will hurt you.' I *hope*, he added silently.

'I know that,' a familiar voice said crossly, 'but I am not the enemy.'

William peered into the shadows. 'Brother Walter?' he asked in astonishment.

The hob crawled to the edge of the bed and sat there, a small, dishevelled figure in the firelight, picking bits of thatch out of his fur.

'What are you doing here?' William stepped over the fire-pit and crouched down in front of him. 'And how did you know where to find me?'

'It was not difficult. Pig smell is easy to track,' the hob said, wrinkling his nose. 'I came to warn you that Shadlok followed you from the abbey today. I lost him in the place of the cut trees.'

'The hazel coppice,' William said, nodding. 'Are you sure he was coming after me? He might just have been looking for food. Master Bone said they would see to their own needs.'

The hob shook his head. 'Shadlok has no need for food. Not mortal food. Nor has Master Bone. He was following you.'

157

'He hasn't come near the hut,' William said, but then he thought, *how would I know if he had*? He might be out there now, listening at the door. 'Master Bone was asking questions about the angel earlier today. I told him I knew nothing about it, but I don't think either of them believed me. Perhaps Shadlok wants to get me on my own and force me to tell him what I know.'

The hob looked thoughtful as he took this in. 'Most curious. The Dark King kills the nangel, Shadlok and Bone are age-old enemies of the king, and Bone wants to find out more about the nangel.' He drew a circle in the air with his finger. 'It goes round and around, all joined together.'

'But there are pieces missing,' William said, 'because it still doesn't make any sense to me.'

He added some branches to the fire. He was glad to see the hob and was touched that Brother Walter had cared enough about him to come to the hut and warn him about Shadlok.

'I hammered nails around the door,' William said. 'They are not going to keep Shadlok out, are they?' He glanced up at the roof. Stars showed through the gap in the thatch.

The hob shook his head. 'No. His magic is too strong.'

'So what do we do now?

The hob settled himself by the fire pit. He wrapped his arms and tail tightly around his body. 'We wait and see what happens.'

For a while, William put his ear to the door and listened for any slight noise outside the hut, but nothing disturbed the silence. At last tiredness overtook him and he yawned loudly.

'You go to sleep,' the hob said. 'I will keep watch.'

William opened his mouth to argue, but the hob waved an impatient paw at him. 'There is no sense in both of us staying awake.'

'Very well,' William said, yawning again. 'But wake me if you need me.'

He lay down on the bed and closed his eyes, and within moments he was asleep.

When he woke again, it felt as if only minutes had passed, but the gap in the thatch now showed a patch of pale-blue sky. He rolled onto his back and stretched sleepily.

The hob was adding wood to the fire and the last of yesterday's bread was warming on a stone on the edge of the pit. He was humming softly to himself and his tufted ears twitched as he listened to the early morning birdsong.

'Was it a quiet night?' William asked, sitting up and pushing aside the blanket covering him. He swung his legs over the side of the bed frame.

'I am not sure . . .' The hob frowned and glanced at the door. 'There was something out there for a time. It passed the hut several times but did not pause. I don't think it could see the hut.'

William smiled uncertainly. 'What do you mean? How could anyone miss it? It was a clear night and the moon is coming up to full.'

'Somebody hid it.'

William stared down at the hob, baffled. 'How?'

'By deceiving the eyes with deep fay magic. Hiding it in plain sight by casting a glamour over it. Disguising it as a tree, maybe, or a rock.'

'Who would do that? And why?'

The hob shrugged a shoulder. 'I do not know, but I sensed a very old and powerful magic at work. It seems we have a friend out there.'

William opened the door and looked out. A thin mist shimmered between the oaks in the early morning light. Somewhere nearby a robin sang. The pigs grunted and rustled in their shelter, impatient to be let out to forage. A fox stood on the far side of the stream, watching him. William started to turn away, then paused. There was something about the animal's eyes . . .

'Brother Walter?' William called softly, not taking his eyes from the fox. 'Come here, quickly.'

'What is it?' the hob asked.

'Over there. The fox,' he murmured.

He heard the hob draw a sharp breath and glanced down at him. The hob's eyes were narrowed as he stared at the animal and the fur along his spine bristled.

'It's not really a fox, is it?' William said, already knowing the answer.

The hob did not reply. William could sense the tension in the creature's body and wondered if they were in danger.

He felt inside the cuff of his jacket for the four-leaved clover. What had Brother Snail told him? It would let him see through fay glamour, to see a fay creature in its true form. But the clover had gone. It must have fallen out during the night.

The fox walked forward. It hesitated by the water's edge for a moment, then crossed the stream, stepping quickly and seeming to barely touch the water. It walked up the slope towards the hut. William's first instinct was to go back inside and bar the door, but the hob stood his ground, so William did not move.

The fox stopped a few paces away. Closer to, William could see that its eyes were not the usual golden brown of a fox's eyes, but a pale winter blue. In that moment he knew who the animal really was.

The air around the fox shimmered like a heat haze rising from warm stone. Afterwards William could not remember if he had seen the animal's body actually change shape and grow, but one moment he was staring at a fox, and the next he was looking into the strange, cold eyes of the fay, Shadlok.

Chapter Seventeen

'You know what I am?' Shadlok asked, looking at William. The fay was armed; a sword and long-bladed knife hung from his belt, and there was a bow and a quiver of arrows on his back.

William nodded. He glanced down at the hob. 'He told me. You're a Seelie fay, from the court of Queen Yarael.'

A fleeting look of pain crossed the fay's scarred face. 'That was a long time ago.'

'What do you want with me?' William asked. 'You followed me here, so you must want something.'

'You know full well what I want.'

The words, spoken softly, sent a chill through William's chest.

'You want me to help you find the hill in the drawings. I already told you, I don't know where it is.'

'Lie to me and it will be the last thing you do,' Shadlok said. 'You know about the angel.' It was not a question.

William swallowed a couple of times, his throat suddenly dry and tight, but he lifted his chin and looked the fay in the eye. Inside, he was shaking with fear, but outside, he tried to appear calm. 'A little,' he admitted.

'At last, we are getting somewhere,' Shadlok said. He glanced down at the small dishevelled figure of the hob. There were still bits of thatch in the creature's fur. 'Do you trust this mortal?'

'He saved my life.' The hob was visibly trembling.

'But do you *trust* him?'

The hob nodded. William smiled briefly, oddly touched by this.

Shadlok suddenly stiffened and for a moment he seemed to be listening to something that William could not hear. He turned quickly and stared into the woodland, his pale eyes wide and his expression sharp and alert.

'Into the hut,' he ordered. 'Now.'

William did not argue. The hob limped ahead of him but hesitated for a moment by the doorway, as if reluctant to go through. He took a deep breath and hunched his shoulders up to his ears. He almost threw himself through the doorway and scuttled over to crouch down in a corner of the room.

William stood by the fire-pit and watched as Shadlok closed and barred the hut door. There was a tightness around his mouth and William noticed he flinched when he touched the door. It seemed the iron nails were doing their work.

William opened his mouth to ask what was happening, but the fay held up a hand to silence him.

Shadlok closed his eyes. His lips moved as if he was speaking, but he made no sound. He raised his hands, palms out towards the door, and stood like that for the next few minutes.

William looked down at the hob with a questioning frown, but the hob's full attention was on Shadlok. There was a look of terror on the creature's face, but William did not know if it was because of the fay's strange behaviour, or if something else had frightened him.

The atmosphere in the hut began to change. The smoky air freshened and grew colder. William felt an uncomfortable prickling sensation where it touched his bare skin.

At last, Shadlok lowered his arms and the tension

left his body. He turned to look at William.

'You are not safe in these woods. You should go back to the abbey.'

'I can't,' William said. 'I was told to bring the pigs here to forage for acorns. The prior will be angry if I disobey him and return before he sends for me.'

The fay's eyes flashed with sudden anger. 'You would prefer a slow and painful death to a few hard words from your prior?'

William stared at him. When had death of any kind, painful or otherwise, been mentioned?

'Is that a threat?' William managed to ask, his throat tightening.

'A warning,' Shadlok said, with a touch of impatience. He nodded to the hut door. 'Out there, now, are creatures who would not think twice about peeling the skin from your body with their nails and teeth while you are still alive. They would rip the beating heart from your chest and smile while they did it. Do you fear your prior more than you fear them?'

William, unable to speak, shook his head. Behind him, the hob whimpered softly.

'I have hidden the hut from their eyes twice, but they can sense human blood close by and are suspicious. They have moved deeper into the wood and for now you are safe, but they will be back. We do not have much time. Tell me what you know about the angel. Help me now and I will answer all your questions later.'

William struggled to control the fear rising inside him. 'Whatever is out there is after you, not us. They followed you to the abbey.'

'You think that will stop them from killing you?' the fay said softly, a grim smile just touching his mouth. 'They are creatures of the Dark King. Killing is in their nature.'

William decided he had no choice but to trust Shadlok. The fay had just saved his life, after all.

Hesitantly at first, William told the fay what little he knew, about the angel's death in the snow and its secret burial on Christmas Eve, a hundred years ago. 'The hill you are looking for,' he finished, hoping he was not making a terrible mistake, 'I think it is Gremanhil, north of the track to Yagleah.'

'Is that where the angel is buried?'

'I don't know,' William said. He saw the fay's eyes narrow and added quickly, 'I really don't know. I think there are clues in the drawings, though.'

'Such as?'

'The sheep behind the angel in the first picture,

that means Sheep Brook, on the road to Yagleah, where the angel's body was found. The crows are for Crowfield Abbey, but you must have known that or you wouldn't be here.'

Shadlok said nothing. He waited for William to continue.

'I don't know what the acorn or the hazelnut mean. If they give clues to the whereabouts of the grave, then it could be just about anywhere. Half of the trees in Foxwist Wood are either oaks or hazels.'

It was hard to say if Shadlok was disappointed by this or if William had merely told him what he already knew.

'The angel saved a hob from the Dark King,' Shadlok said, 'but the creature does not appear in the drawings, so how did you find out about it?'

William hesitated. He glanced at Brother Walter. 'He told me.'

The hob stood up, grabbing a corner of William's jacket to steady himself. 'The Old Red Man was a hob, like me, but he was a house fay, not like me. The king hung him from a tree and his followers started beating him with the flat of their swords. They cut off his tail.' The hob's voice quavered and he paused for a moment. 'The nangel came out of the hillside and cut him free. The king was angry and shot the nangel with an arrow.'

William looked down at the hob, startled. 'Out of the *hillside*? Out of Gremanhil?'

The hob nodded. 'There was a bright light and the hillside opened, and there was the nangel. So the Old Red Man told me and he had no reason to lie.'

William thought for a moment. It explained why Shadlok and Master Bone were so interested in the hill.

But it didn't make any sense. What was an angel doing inside Gremanhil?

A faint smile touched the corners of Shadlok's mouth. William had the feeling the fay was pleased by what the hob had told him. He also knew he would be wasting his breath asking why that was.

'This hob, where is he now?' Shadlok asked.

The hob hesitated for a moment. 'In a house in Weforde, the last I heard of him.'

'Perhaps he saw where the monks buried the angel,' Shadlok said.

'He hid until the Dark King had gone. He saw the monks carry the nangel away, but he did not follow them. He had lost much blood and was in pain and there was nothing he could do to help the nangel, one way or the other.'

'Which way did they go? Was it towards Yagleah or Weforde?' William asked.

The hob shook his head. 'He did not say.'

'Then we must ask him,' Shadlok said. He turned and, after the briefest hesitation, opened the door. He stepped outside and glanced back at William and the hob.

'Well? What are you waiting for?'

'You want us to come with you?' William asked, startled.

'Unless you would prefer to be here alone when the Dark King's warriors return, then you will be safer with me.'

'But I can't just leave the pigs,' William said.

'Then stay,' Shadlok said coldly. 'It is your choice. But the hob comes with me.'

The hob shook his head and whimpered softly. He looked up at William with fear-filled eyes.

William thought quickly. He could not let Shadlok take the hob, and Mary Magdalene and the two pigs would be safe enough in their pen for the next few hours. 'If I go with you, will you come back here with me afterwards?'

The fay nodded. 'I will escort you to the abbey.'

William decided he would worry about what to say to the prior later. But however angry the prior might be at William's disobedience, he would sooner take his chances with Prior Ardo than the Dark King; at least the prior was not likely to skin William with his nails and teeth, or rip his heart out.

'Very well,' William said, nodding. He saw the look of relief on the hob's face. William followed Brother Walter to the hut door. Something small and whitish lay on the floor, half hidden beneath a frond of dried bracken. He leant down and picked it up. It was the fold of parchment with the four-leafed clover still tucked inside. It must have fallen from his sleeve when he jumped out of bed earlier. He pushed it back inside the cuff of his sleeve.

William took the pig-stick from where it was propped against the hut wall and nodded towards the steam. 'Weforde is that way.'

Ignoring the hopeful grunts from the pigs, and with a wary glance around the clearing and the wintry woods beyond, he set off after the two fays.

The hob limped along, his face tight with pain, and quickly fell behind. William went back for him and lifted him onto his shoulders. Shadlok waited for them to catch up with barely concealed impatience, then turned and continued on his way. He looked around all the time, eyes sharp and watchful. He took the bow from his back and carried it in his hand, as if ready for trouble. His brown jacket, tunic and trousers blended with the woodland colours around him, and his silver-white hair gleamed like a shaft of sunlight through the branches.

Even though he was walking just a few paces behind the fay, William found it curiously difficult to see him, and at times, Shadlok seemed to disappear altogether. If he had not known the fay was there, he might not have noticed him at all.

'Why is it,' William asked the hob, keeping his voice down, 'that he doesn't mind people knowing *his* name? You wouldn't tell me yours, because it would give me a hold over you. Why is it different for him?'

'There are few fays more powerful than him,' the hob said softly. 'Merely knowing his name would not help you against him.'

They reached the park pale and climbed the bank to a gap in the sagging wattle fence.

'Weforde is an hour's walk this way,' William said, pointing to a narrow path leading down into a stand of young oaks.

Shadlok glanced at him over his shoulder, a look of

contempt on his face. 'I know.'

'I'm only trying to help,' William muttered, glaring at the fay's back.

'The day I need the help of a human to find my way through woodland, or indeed anywhere else, is the day I will lie down and die,' Shadlok said.

William felt his face grow hot with mingled anger and embarrassment. Of course Shadlok didn't need his help, but he didn't have to be so unpleasant about it. The hob patted William's cheek in silent sympathy.

Shadlok set off between the trees, moving quickly. William had to walk and sprint in turns just to keep up. The hob grabbed his ears and clung on.

'Can you please let go?' William said, trying to shake the hob's paws free.

The hob put his paws on William's forehead instead, which was marginally better, though he managed to poke William in the eye a couple of times as he bounced around during one of their faster sprints after Shadlok.

The hob patted William's head and leant forward to whisper in his ear. 'Why are Shadlok and Master Bone trying to find out where the nangel was buried, do you think?'

William had been wondering about that, too. 'I

173

don't know. Unless they mean to dig it up,' he said. He made the suggestion flippantly, but as soon as he said it, the appalling possibility that this was exactly what they intended to do hit him like a hammer blow. 'They couldn't really mean to do that, surely?'

'Perhaps they want to grind its bones down to make a spell,' the hob said. He rubbed his paw in a circle through William's hair. 'Grindy, grindy. Round and round, strong fay magic.'

'Stop doing that!' William grabbed the hob's good leg and shook it. 'What kind of spell?'

'One that will cure Master Bone of the sickness that eats his flesh. Perhaps the bones of a nangel are magic enough to do that.'

He gazed at Shadlok, walking a little way ahead and hopefully out of earshot. It made sense, he thought, after considering the possibility for several moments. He could not blame Master Bone for wanting to try and find a cure, but was *any* magic strong enough to make his fingers grow back again?

The early morning mist still drifted in hollows and hung over the brackish water of a pond near a charcoal burner's hut. Wood smoke hazed the cold air between the trees and somewhere in the distance, William could hear voices and the sound of someone chopping wood.

They reached the track to Weforde and turned west. The track was broad and if they kept to the edges, away from the deep muddy ruts, the ground was firm and the walking was easy.

'The fays following you,' William said when he caught up with Shadlok, 'are they trying to kill you?'

'No,' Shadlok said.

'So what do they want with you?'

'They are merely watching where I go.'

'Why?'

Shadlok frowned and there was a trace of impatience in his voice when he spoke. 'The Dark King likes to know the whereabouts of his enemies at all times.'

'Where is the king? Is he somewhere close by?'

'I do not know.'

'Doesn't that leave you at a disadvantage?' William persisted. 'He knows where to find you, but you don't know where he is?'

'Just stop talking!' Shadlok snapped, turning to glare at William. 'Humans! You always have to be talking, even when you have nothing to say. I told you, I will answer your questions when we find the angel. Until then, keep *silent*.'

The fay walked on ahead. William pulled a face

behind his back and stuck out his tongue. It was hard to like Shadlok and harder still to understand him. What William could not puzzle out was why, if Shadlok was such a powerful fay, did he choose to be the servant of a human, albeit an immortal one, when he clearly despised humans?

There were dark undercurrents here that William found disturbing. All he knew for sure was that he would be very glad indeed when Master Bone and Shadlok left Crowfield Abbey for good.

Chapter Eighteen

The track left the trees and crested a low hill overlooking Weforde village and its three huge fields. They spread across the valley floor, the smaller individual strips showing as patches of green and brown. The village was a scatter of thatched buildings set squarely in their crofts on either side of the main village street. At the far end of the village, beyond the large square green with its duck pond and pinfold, stood Sir Robert de Tovei's stone manor house, with the newly built stone church beside it.

'Where does the Old Red Man live?' William asked, lifting the hob down from his shoulders.

The hob looked away and it was several moments before he answered. 'In the house of the woman with the white crow, but I do not know where that is.'

William stared at him in astonishment. 'He lives in

177

Dame Alys's house?'

The hob nodded.

'Why didn't you mention this before?' William asked, an uneasy feeling prickling across the back of his neck. There was something not quite right here, but he could not put his finger on what it was. 'Surely that means Dame Alys knows about the angel? The hob must have told her, if only to explain what happened to his tail.'

The hob, keeping his back turned, just shrugged. Again, William had the distinct feeling that there was something the hob was not telling him about Dame Alys.

'What does it matter?' Shadlok said with a frown. His patience, what little there was of it, was wearing very thin indeed.

'She has no love for the monks at Crowfield,' William said slowly, 'so why, if she knew they'd buried the angel's body in the wood, didn't she tell anyone? She must have known what trouble it would have caused for them. Why did she keep their secret when she hates them so much? It doesn't make any sense.'

'Then stop wasting time worrying about it,' Shadlok said. 'Ask her for yourself when we find her.'

William looked at the two fays and a problem

presented itself. Shadlok looked passably human, but the hob would not fool anybody.

'We can't risk anyone seeing you,' he said to the hob.

'They will only see me if they have the Sight,' the hob said, 'and very few humans do.'

'Even so, it's not worth taking the chance,' William said.

'Then they will not see him,' Shadlok said.

William watched in disbelief as the air around the hob shimmered and the hob faded away.

'What have you done with him?' he asked in alarm.

'I am still here,' the hob said.

William reached down and felt the hob, still standing where he had last seen him, as warm and solid as ever.

'Satisfied?' Shadlok asked, with a trace of sarcasm.

William nodded. To see such magic so effortlessly performed left him feeling breathless and a little fearful.

They followed the track as it curved down from the hill and cut across the West Field. In some of the strips, the rise and fall of furrows and ridges were showing the first green haze of winter wheat. Other strips were bare ploughed earth, spread with clods of manure. Crows wheeled up from the field like smuts of soot, cawing loudly, as they passed by.

There were a few people about, busy around their crofts and closes, tending to livestock or just talking over fences, passing the time of day. The blacksmith was hammering a glowing piece of iron, the fire in his forge burning fiercely red behind him.

Several curious glances came their way, but most people recognised William and merely nodded as he passed by. Shadlok had spent three weeks as a guest of Sir William, but if any of the villagers knew who he was, they gave no sign of it. They stared at him, openly suspicious. A man on foot, armed with a sword and bow, was not a sight you saw every day in Weforde. They did not ask what business he had in the village, but William heard the hushed voices behind them as they walked by. They were no doubt wondering what the boy from the abbey was doing in Weforde with an armed stranger.

William spotted Ralph Saddler, a man he often saw at Weforde market. Ralph made and repaired harnesses, straps and saddles, and usually did a brisk trade. Today, he was mending the handle of a scythe. William stopped by the gate of his croft. Ralph glanced up and nodded to him.

'Hello, Will. What brings you to Weforde this morning? It's not market day.'

'I'm looking for Dame Alys's house. Brother Snail at the abbey needs some herbs for a potion for the abbot,' he lied, thinking quickly. 'He hoped that she might be able to help.'

'Hmm,' Ralph said, frowning. 'I see. And who's he?' He nodded towards Shadlok.

'His name is Shadlok. He's staying at the abbey with his master, Jacobus Bone,' William said.

A look of understanding crossed Ralph's face. 'Oh, that's right, the leper.'

Shadlok said nothing. He stared at the man, who seemed to find the pale eyes as unsettling as William did. Ralph looked away and busied himself rolling down his sleeves and brushing bits of sawdust from his tunic.

'Has the track through the woods become so dangerous that you need to carry so many weapons?' Ralph asked, glancing at Shadlok.

'I was hunting. With the prior's permission.'

'Hunting?' Ralph's eyes narrowed. 'With a *sword*?'

Shadlok did not reply. His stare was cold and unblinking. He did not like being questioned and seemed to have no intention of justifying his choice of hunting weapon to the villager.

Ralph looked back at William. 'You'll find Dame Alys's house along the lane past the mill. Across the green, past the alehouse, then over the bridge and up towards Frog Pond Wood. Can't miss it.'

William nodded his thanks. He felt something touch his leg and glanced down. He could not see anything, but he felt the hob climb up his body and settle on his shoulders. Thankfully, Ralph did not notice anything unusual.

William and Shadlok walked towards the green. Keeping his voice low, William said, 'He didn't know who you were.'

'So?'

'You stayed in the village for three weeks, and you asked people about the angel, yet nobody seems to recognise you. That's very odd, isn't it?'

'They did not see me as I am now,' Shadlok said with a dismissive lift of one shoulder. 'They saw what I wanted them to see.'

More fay magic, William thought. He shivered suddenly. His few brief glimpses of Shadlok's power were enough to make him exceedingly wary of the fay. He could take another shape, another face, with the same ease with which William changed his clothing.

An alehouse stood on one corner of the green. A wooden board painted with a sprig of holly hung from a bracket near the door. The malty smell of brewing beer and the tantalising waft of freshly baked bread made William's mouth water as he walked by. Hunger gnawed in his belly and he tried not to think about food.

In the middle of the green, beside the duck-pond, was the pinfold, a fenced enclosure where stray animals were penned until they could be claimed by their owners, upon payment of a small fine to the pinder. This morning, the only occupants were a goat and two chickens.

They walked along the lane to the bridge over the stream. The lane branched in two on the far bank. They turned left and followed the lane as far as the water mill before turning onto a narrower path, which led to a small wood. Hidden away behind a hedge of holly bushes was a small house surrounded by a well-tended garden. The few remaining holly berries left by the birds were like drops of blood amongst the dark leaves. Smoke drifted up from a hole in the thatched roof of the house.

William helped the hob down from his shoulders. 'What if Dame Alys won't let us talk to the Old Red

Man?'

'There are ways of persuading her,' Shadlok said softly, an icy glitter in his eyes.

William hoped it would not come to that. He had the feeling Shadlok would be ruthless with anyone foolish enough to cross him.

A path of flat stones led between rows of cabbages and leeks, and past manured beds waiting for the spring planting. The white crow, Fionn, was standing by the hut door. It watched them as they walked up the path. Leaning forward, it cawed once, a loud, harsh noise in the quiet garden. The hut door opened and Dame Alys stood there. She looked from William to Shadlok calmly, then glanced down at the crow and said, 'Leave them be.'

The bird moved aside with an ungainly hop and flapped up to sit on top of a water butt.

Dame Alys stepped out of the hut and rested her hands on her thin hips. Her gaze briefly flickered to the path by William's feet. 'What is it you want with me, William Paynel?'

William cleared his throat, not sure how to explain why they had come to see her. 'Eh . . . well, I was told you have a hob living here with you. The Old Red Man?'

She waited for him to continue, her oddly coloured eyes sharp and watchful.

'We were wondering if we could ask him something.'

'And what would that be?'

William hesitated for a moment, unsure of how much he should tell her. 'He saw something in the woods, one Christmas Eve many years ago. We want to know what he remembers of that night.'

'I see.' Dame Alys regarded Shadlok thoughtfully for a few moments. 'And who are you?'

'Shadlok, servant to Master Jacobus Bone.' He said the words coldly with a look in his eyes that William did not like. Anyone less like a servant than Shadlok was difficult to imagine but Dame Alys did not seem in the least bit intimidated by him. William felt a flicker of admiration for her.

'Fine weapons for a manservant,' she said, nodding to the sword and knife in Shadlok's belt. Her eyes narrowed slightly. 'And so unusual. If I didn't know better, I would say they were of fay workmanship.'

Shadlok remained silent. William glanced from the woman to the fay, aware of the tension in the air between them. He wondered how she knew what fay workmanship looked like. It seemed it was not just hobs she was familiar with.

'Perhaps,' Dame Alys said, turning to William, 'you can tell me why you brought a fay to my house.' She glanced at the path again. 'And a hob.'

'You can see him? Brother Walter?' William said, surprised.

'Is that what you have called him?' she said sharply, not sounding at all pleased by this.

William nodded.

'No, I can't see him but I can sense him. I'll ask you again, why are they here with you? And what was it that happened in the woods that you are so keen to learn more about?'

This was a lot more difficult than he had anticipated. William made some noncommittal noise and shrugged one shoulder.

'That is none of your concern,' Shadlok said, a warning edge to his voice.

'Something puzzles me, William,' Dame Alys said, ignoring Shadlok. 'I have the Sight, and I can see hobs and other fay creatures, but I cannot see the hob you brought with you. Now, why is that? It would take stronger magic than such a creature possesses to hide it from me. That begs the question, whose magic is it? Not yours, I am sure,' she added, gently mocking.

She looked at Shadlok. 'Yours, perhaps? You are no ordinary fay, then, to be able to do this. To hide it from *me*.'

Still Shadlok said nothing. He moved a hand and the air by William's feet shimmered and darkened, and the hob was there, solid and whole again.

Dame Alys turned and walked to her door. 'William, you and the hob can come into the house but the fay must stay outside.'

William glanced uncertainly at Shadlok, half expecting him to refuse, but he merely nodded for William to follow Dame Alys.

'Keep watch, Fionn,' Dame Alys called as she went inside. The crow hopped onto the path outside the door as if to guard it from Shadlok. It could not have been made plainer that the fay was not welcome there.

William leant the pig-stick against the bench and went through the low doorway.

The house consisted of one room, with a ladder up to a sleeping loft beneath the thatched roof. Bundles of dried plants hung from the rafters and jars of various sizes crowded the shelves that lined two walls. There was a fire pit in the middle, surrounded by a hearth of pitched clay tiles. A soot-blackened pot stood on an iron trivet set squarely amongst the embers. Something bubbled and steamed in the pot and smelled so wonderful that William's mouth began to water. It reminded him of his mother's pease pottage, with a hint of smoked pork for flavour. Just for a moment it felt as if he was back home in the mill house in Iwele, sitting at the table with his noisy, happy family, while his mother ladled pottage into bowls. A sharp sense of loss caught him off guard and tears blurred his eyes.

He blinked them away, pushed the memory of home to the back of his mind and looked around the room. It was clean and as neatly ordered as the garden, with a long oak table, a chair and a stool, and a large cupboard providing the only furniture. Fresh straw covered the beaten earth floor.

'Are you hungry, William?' Dame Alys asked.

William nodded, trying not to look too eager.

'Sit at the table. You can have a bowl of pottage while your hob and mine talk.'

William looked uncertainly towards the door. 'What about Shadlok?'

'The fay can wait for you. It might do him some good to learn a little patience.'

William grinned and pulled the stool up to the table. He wouldn't argue with that.

The pottage was every bit as good as it smelled. It was well seasoned with herbs and thick with chunks of smoked pork. *This must be what it's like to die and go to heaven*, William thought, slowly chewing a piece of meat and letting the rich, smoky taste fill his mouth.

Dame Alys put a piece of freshly baked white wheat bread on the table by his bowl. She gave another piece to the hob, who was watching her hopefully from the bottom rung of the loft ladder.

A small head poked through the opening in the loft floor and two large eyes glittered red in the light from the fire. William watched as a thin creature, not unlike Brother Walter, but with longer, redder fur, climbed slowly down the ladder. Its face was as wrinkled as last year's apples. Its body was hunched and bent and its tail was just a stump. The Old Red Man was aptly named.

The two hobs greeted each other like the long-lost friends they were, chittering and whistling excitedly in a curious language all of their own. William wondered if Dame Alys understood what they were saying. He would not have been surprised if she did.

William dipped a crust of bread into the pottage and put it into his mouth. It was the best meal he had eaten since he had left Iwele.

'Why are you searching for the angel's grave?' Dame Alys asked, sitting down across the table from him.

William choked on the bread and it was a few minutes before he could talk again. 'You know about the angel?'

The woman nodded. 'Of course I do. What do you want with it?'

William was reluctant to say more than he had to. He was not sure if he could trust Dame Alys.

'Ah!' A look of understanding came into her eyes. 'Of course, it's not *you*; it's the fay who is looking for the grave.' Her mouth hardened. 'I knew someone had been asking questions in the village. It was him. Why is he so desperate to find it, William?'

William shifted uncomfortably under the woman's unblinking gaze. 'I think . . . I think he wants to use its bones in a healing spell. For his master, Jacobus Bone.'

To his astonishment, Dame Alys started to laugh. Her mouth widened amongst a maze of wrinkles and her body shook. Her laugh was like the harsh grate of rusty iron hinges and her eyes were bright with malice. She spread her thin fingers on the table and rocked back and forth on her stool. William stared at her uneasily, wondering what was so funny.

'You live in a world of fools, of monks and fays. You should choose your friends with more care, boy. They will lead you a merry dance to the gates of hell.'

William put his spoon down. His appetite had deserted him. What was the woman talking about?

William pushed his chair back and got to his feet. 'Thank you for the food, but I think we should be going.' His voice sounded strange to his own ears.

'As you like,' Dame Alys said with a shrug. She left the table and crossed to the door, where she stood with her hand on the latch.

William brushed the crumbs from the front of his jacket. The movement dislodged the piece of parchment from his cuff. He caught it as it fell, and the four-leafed clover slipped out onto his palm. His hand tingled as if he had brushed against a nettle. Around him the room seemed to darken and he saw, for a brief moment, a figure in the shadows beside the cupboard. It was wrapped in a tattered grey cloak and wore a mummer's mask in the shape of a long-beaked bird, a heron, perhaps.

William gasped and his fist clenched, crushing the clover leaf to dust. The figure disappeared. The room became lighter and everything was as it had been before.

'Did you see it?' he said, his voice catching in his throat. 'Over there, in the corner?'

Dame Alys was watching him. Her eyes, one blue, one brown, were wide and bright. He could see the white line around her tightly closed lips. She did not answer him. She opened the door and stood aside to let him leave.

William stared into the corner beside the cupboard. He had the uneasy feeling that the bird-headed figure was still there, though he could not see anything.

'What was it?' he asked.

'I didn't see anything,' she said stiffly, her stare unblinking.

'There was someone over there, wearing a mask,' William insisted, but Dame Alys did not let him finish.

'The firelight plays tricks with the shadows,' she said softly. 'You saw nothing.'

He opened his mouth to argue, but then closed it again. He knew he would be wasting his breath. The hob hurried over to him and together they left the house. The door closed behind them.

'Did you see it? The figure in the bird mask?' William asked, glancing down at the hob.

The hob nodded. His eyes were wide and full of fear. 'It was a bad thing, a shadow-thing,' he whispered.

'What was it? Do you know?'

The hob hesitated. He looked nervously over his shoulder at the shuttered window of the hut as if worried that he would be overheard. 'I saw something like it, a long time ago, in the grove of oaks by the Hunter's Tree. Back in the time before strangers from over the sea came to the forest and built the straight stone track, people would make offerings to the spirit there, a shadow-thing with a bird's head.'

'A holy grove?' William said, puzzled. 'Where?'

The hob shook his head. 'It is gone, cut down and burned. I thought the shadow-thing had gone too, but now I am not so sure.'

With a last glance back at the hut, William walked to the gate. The hob hurried ahead of him, clearly anxious to be away from whatever it was they had seen.

Shadlok was waiting for them in the lane, arms folded and pacing back and forth impatiently. Fionn was perched on a fence post nearby, watching the fay beadily.

'Well?' Shadlok said sharply. He did not look

pleased at having been made to wait so long. 'What did you find out?' He peered more closely at William's face. 'What happened in there?'

'We saw something,' William said. Quickly, he told Shadlok about the bird-headed figure.

Shadlok said nothing for a few moments but there was a thoughtful look in his eyes. 'The bird head was a mask, you say?'

William nodded. 'I think so.'

The fay said something softly in a language William did not understand. It sounded like a name, but William could not be sure. The white crow rose into the air with a loud caw and a sudden clap of its wings that made William jump. It flapped up to sit on the roof of Dame Alys's hut, where it continued to call angrily, as if at any moment it might swoop down and attack them.

'What's the matter with him?' William said.

Shadlok smiled grimly. 'The bird has secrets to guard. It does not want us here.'

William wondered what Shadlok had said that had sent it into such a rage.

'So what was it,' William asked, 'the thing in the hut?'

'Something you would be wise to stay as far away

from as you can.' Shadlok said with a finality that made William think twice about questioning him any further.

The fay looked down at the hob. 'What did you find out from the Red Man?' he asked.

'He said the brother men carried the nangel along the track towards *this* village,' the hob said, keeping a wary eye on the white crow.

'What else did he tell you?'

'That the king cut off his tail.' The hob made a slicing movement with his paw. 'Chop, tail gone.'

Shadlok's eyes narrowed. 'I meant, about the angel.'

The hob bristled with indignation. 'A hob's tail is his greatest pride.'

Shadlok stared at the hob in silence.

'That was all he said,' the hob added with a lift of one shoulder, looking away.

'Hobs,' Shadlok said with biting contempt. 'I should have known we would be wasting our time.'

William hid a smile. With a quick flick of his hand, Shadlok made the hob disappear again. For one worried moment, William wondered if the fay had done something more sinister, but a paw grabbed the leg of his hose and he felt the hob climb up onto his shoulders.

William was in a thoughtful mood as they walked back to the village. He was puzzled and unsettled by the figure he had glimpsed in the hut. It was not a creature of flesh and blood, so what was it? And what was it doing in Dame Alys's house?

Dame Alys's appearance as an old woman who made salves and caudles was deceptive. William had the feeling that she was dangerous; she knew too much and saw too much. It might be prudent to keep away from her from now on.

Chapter Nineteen

Shadlok walked on ahead of William and the hob. He was not in a good mood and William decided that keeping some distance between them was probably for the best, so he slowed down and soon fell a little way behind.

Ralph Saddler walked over to his gate when he saw William coming along the village street.

'Wasn't Dame Alys able to help you then, lad?' he called. 'Needed some herbs, didn't you?'

'No, she didn't have any to spare,' William lied, shaking his head. The movement unsettled the hob, who grabbed William's ears to steady himself. William grunted in surprise, but quickly turned it into a cough. Ralph peered at him curiously.

'You all right, young Will?'

'Yes, fine,' William muttered, feeling his cheeks redden. The hob's grip on his ears tightened as he tried to settle more securely on William's shoulders.

'Sorry,' the hob murmured, his breath tickling William's ear.

William coughed again, louder this time, hoping Ralph had not heard the hob. He started to edge away from the saddler, not wanting to stop and talk. Shadlok was already partway across the West Field and showed no signs of slowing down to wait for him.

Ralph leant on the gate, his large hands resting on the wooden bar. He nodded towards Shadlok. 'He's a strange 'un, isn't he? What do you make of him?'

'I barely know him. He only came to Crowfield a couple of days ago.' William took another step away from the gate.

'You've seen that master of his? The leper?' Ralph asked. He seemed set for a long gossip. William tried to hide his impatience and merely nodded. He liked Ralph, but the saddler could talk the back legs off an ox. That was all right if it was market day and you were just standing around, but William did not have time for this today. He did not want to walk back through Foxwist with just the hob for company, and he was not at all sure Shadlok would wait for him.

'Can't imagine why anyone would choose to serve a leper,' Ralph went on, shaking his head, 'unless they were very holy and good, or the leper had a hold over them in some way.'

William could think of several words to describe Shadlok, but *holy* and *good* were not amongst them.

The hob seemed to share William's anxiety to hurry after Shadlok. He started to fidget and squeezed William's ears between his thin little fingers. William jerked his head sideways, almost dislodging the hob.

Ralph looked at him curiously. 'You're sure you're all right, lad? You seem a mite fidgety today.'

'Lice,' William said quickly, scratching his head. The hob joined in, his fingers poking and scratching at William's scalp. William scratched more vigorously, and managed to prod the hob in the stomach in an attempt to make him sit still.

'Well, you'll have to run if you want to catch up with your friend,' Ralph said, straightening up. 'I'll see you next market day.'

William nodded and hurried along the track at an awkward jog. The hob bounced up and down on his shoulders, his paws holding tightly to William's hair.

'What did you think you were *doing*?' William hissed angrily. 'Another few moments and Ralph Saddler would have thought I was possessed, jigging around like that.'

'What is *pessest*?' the hob asked breathlessly. In spite of the discomfort of his bony haunches digging into William's shoulders, he seemed to be quite enjoying the bumpy ride.

'It's when a demon lives inside you and takes over your body and thoughts, and makes you do strange things.'

'Like squirrels,' the hob said.

'Squirrels?' William said, baffled. 'How is being possessed like squirrels?'

'They do strange things,' the hob said darkly. 'They take over your burrow and your food store. They are pessest.'

William grinned. Demon squirrels in Foxwist? After the last few days, he was ready to believe almost anything was possible.

Up ahead, Shadlok had reached the slope in the track leading up into the forest. William was relieved to see him stop and turn to look back. Even at that distance, he could sense the fay's impatience as he waited for William and the hob to catch up with him.

As he trudged along the track, William went over in his mind what little they knew about the night the angel had died. It would have taken two, perhaps three hours to carry a body from the Sheep Brook ford to Weforde in the snow. The monks could have buried the angel anywhere along the track's length. Short of digging up the entire wood, there was no way of knowing where the grave was.

William thought hard. He was missing something here. If the monk had put clues to the site of the grave, then it meant the grave could be found by anyone who could work out what the clues meant. A hazelnut and an acorn. What would make those two particular trees stand out from countless others in the wood?

'Did the Red Man remember anything else at all?' William asked the hob at last.

'He heard one of the brother men say he knew a safe place to bury the body. He said the stories would keep people away so nobody would ever find it.'

'The stories?' William said, puzzled. 'What stories?'

'I asked him that but he did not know.'

Come on, think! William told himself. A place people told stories about, of the kind that would make them shun it. An oak and a hazel.

A light suddenly seemed to shine in William's mind. Of course! Excitement burned through him and his heart began to beat hard and fast. 'I know where the grave is!'

'You do?' the hob sounded surprised. 'Where?'

'The one place they knew nobody would willingly go near. The Whistling Hollow. The oak in the picture is the Boundary Oak, and the hazel, I'm fairly sure, is the hazel tree growing beside the pool.'

He was certain he was right. There was nowhere else in Foxwist Wood it could be.

'That is a bad place,' the hob said fearfully.

'You know it?'

'All the woodland creatures do. We stay away from it. A bad, *bad* place.'

William felt a shudder go through the hob's body.

'Do you know what haunts the Hollow?' William asked.

'Something old . . .' the hob's voice faded to a whisper. He huddled close to William's head and his breath was warm on William's cheek. 'It watches the woods from the place by the pool and sometimes it walks the woodland paths on winter nights.'

William shivered. He did not like the sound of that. 'Have you ever seen it?'

'I hide when it is walking. All woodlanders do, we stay hidden until it has gone.'

William thought of Brother Gabriel's warning, that the devil hunted for unwary souls in Foxwist. Was the spirit in the hollow the devil? Or was it something else and the monks simply called it the devil because they had no other name for it?

'Are you going to tell Shadlok that you know where the angel is?' the hob asked.

'He will have to tell me why he wants to find the grave first.'

'Nangel bone magic,' the hob said softly. 'Grindy, grindy.'

Chapter Twenty

'You took your time,' Shadlok said when William finally caught up with him.

'If you'd bothered to wait . . .' William began, nettled.

'You might have time to waste gossiping with people, I do not.' Shadlok turned and walked away. William glared at the fay's back.

They walked along in silence. By late morning, the cold, bright day had given way to an overcast sky and a wind from the north. It keened through the branches of the trees in the forest, making them sway and creak overhead, and sent a last few dead leaves skittering across the track. The deep ruts had softened a little, making it muddy underfoot. William stopped every now and then to wipe the worst of the mud from his boots onto the grass on the edge of the track. Shadlok, he noticed, seemed to have no such trouble.

Quite how he managed to keep his boots so clean, William had no idea. Perhaps mud did not stick to fays, he thought.

Shadlok had made the hob visible again. The creature's thin hairy legs and large feet hung down over William's chest. His tail was looped around William's neck and his toes curled and uncurled as he sniffed the air.

'There is snow coming,' the hob said.

William shivered. When winter bit down hard on the land, the abbey seemed to hold the northern chill within its stone walls. Bitter draughts keened under doors and along the cloister alleys, bringing hacking coughs and fevered colds in their wake. He remembered last winter, his first at Crowfield, when the only sound, apart from the regular clang of the bells, was the barking coughs or sneezing of sick monks.

'Where do you live when you're in the woods?' William asked. It was something he had often wondered about.

'I have a burrow deep under the roots of an oak tree,' the hob replied.

'Isn't that cold and damp?'

'No. My burrow is lined with leaves and moss. I keep a store of nuts and berries there, so I do not have to go outside when the rain comes, or if it snows. It is warm and comfortable, and I have the oak tree for company. We talk sometimes.'

William raised his eyebrows. 'You talk to a tree?'

The hob patted William's head. 'In here.'

'What do you talk about?'

'Hob things. And tree things.'

Ask a stupid question, William thought with a wry smile. 'Don't you miss your burrow?'

'Of course, but I like the snail brother's hut too. I am happy to live there for now.'

'Oh, good,' William said with a grin. 'Perhaps when you leave the abbey, I'll come and stay with you in your burrow.'

'I might not have enough nuts to share with you.' There was a note of anxiety in the hob's voice. 'And by now, if I know anything about squirrels – and I *do* – then they have seized their chance to raid my winter store. You cannot trust squirrels,' he added, a hint of a growl in his voice.

William tried not to laugh. 'I think, between us, we are more than a match for a few squirrels. *We'll* raid *their* nut store.'

The hob considered this. 'That might work very well. And we can take their pine cones too. That might make them think again about pelting me from the branches of the trees.'

They left the track and followed a path which wove through a stand of young oaks, each one planted with cleared space around it so they could grow straight and tall. These were Sir Robert's trees, to be cut when he had need of new roof beams or wall timbers.

From there, the path led into a hazel coppice and then curved away into the wildwood, narrowing as it passed between large old oaks and through thorn thickets. Looking up, William saw grey clouds scudding by. There was an edge to the wind that pinched his fingers and toes and hinted at the bitter weather to come.

The path joined a second, wider one that led to the swineherd's hut. Shadlok slowed his pace to allow William and the hob to catch up with him again. His jaw was set and he seemed tense.

'Stay close,' he said softly.

'What's wrong?' William asked.

The fay's sharp gaze swept the undergrowth and he seemed to be listening for something. 'We are being tracked.'

A chill went through William's body. He stared at the fay. 'We are?'

'There are two of them, a little way behind us. They have been following us for a while. Take this, and be prepared to use it.' Shadlok took the knife from his belt and held the hilt towards William.

The knife was light and thin-bladed. William had never seen one like it before. Patterns and letters were etched along the silver blade and the handle was inlaid with tiny pieces of bone in the form of a sinuous, coiling creature.

William tucked the knife into his belt. Apart from play fights with his brother Hugh and the boys in his village, he had never fought anyone with a weapon of any kind.

'Who are they?' William asked anxiously. 'Are they fays? Or outlaws?'

'Does it matter?' Shadlok said. He took the bow from his back and walked away.

William followed quickly, one hand gripping Brother Walter's good leg, the other holding the pig-stick. He wasn't sure which would be worse, coming face to face with a fay warrior, or being attacked by outlaws. Only last August, Hal Brunleggin from Yagleah had been set upon by three men in Foxwist, on his way home from Weforde market. They had stolen his money and his boots, and had left him for dead with a lump the size of a duck's egg on his head.

And what if it came to a fight? Did Shadlok really expect him to use the knife against an armed outlaw? And survive?

Brother Walter wound his fingers into William's hair and his tail coiled around William's neck. William could feel the small body trembling with fear.

'If I need to put you on the ground, run for cover as fast as you can,' William said, tugging at the hob's tail to loosen it a little.

'I will stay and fight,' the hob said, but William heard the quaver in his voice.

'And do what? Bite their knees? Do as I say, and hide.'

William looked around and his heart missed a beat. There was no sign of Shadlok.

'He's gone!' William gasped. 'We're on our own!'

The hob whimpered. William quickened his pace, trying not to panic. His hand gripping the pig-stick was damp with sweat. His breath was harsh in his throat. Underfoot, dead bracken hid tree roots. He stumbled a couple of times but quickly regained his footing. The hob clung to him. William could feel the creature's heart beating like a small drum against his ear.

Something stroked his cheek. There was a sting of pain and a dull thud as an arrow hit a birch tree an arm's span from William's face. He touched his cheek with a trembling finger. Blood. The arrow had grazed his skin.

The hob whimpered. The arrow had nicked him too, but his thick fur had stopped the sharp point from doing more serious damage.

William stared wildly around. It was several moments before he saw a movement away to his right. To his horror, he glimpsed a man fitting an arrow to a bow. Instinctively, he dropped to his knees. The hob tumbled from his shoulders and crawled under a fallen branch, where he hid beneath a tangle of trailing brambles.

'Stay there,' William hissed. 'Don't move.'

The hob huddled into a tight crouch, his face crumpled with terror.

William, keeping low, ran towards a sprawling holly bush. He reached it and straightened up. Peering between the leaves, William could no longer see the archer. He took several deep breaths and threw the pig-stick aside. It would not be of any use against arrows. He took the knife from his belt and held it up in front of him. He was certain the man was close by, waiting for his chance to loose an arrow into William's body.

'You'll have to catch me first,' William muttered through gritted teeth. Moving as quietly as he could, he crept around the holly bush, but the bowman had the advantage, and William knew it. This was not an even fight in any sense, but a fight it would be; William was not going to make this too easy for the man stalking him.

He broke cover and ran towards the hazel coppice, jumping over fallen branches and skidding on brambles, darting from side to side as he went.

A second arrow whistled through the air. This time it missed, but William felt the stir of air as it sliced past his head. His heart hammered against his ribs as he reached the sheltering bulk of a coppiced tree and stood with his shoulders against the trunk.

Away to his right, there was a sudden commotion. William heard the clash of metal on wood, and two figures almost danced into sight. Shadlok swung his bow at a man armed with a sword. The man held the hilt with both hands and hacked at Shadlok's bow. The bow and the sword flashed through the air so fast

William could barely see them. They fought with bewildering speed. It was impossible to make out what was happening or tell who was winning until Shadlok winded his opponent with a well-aimed blow to the stomach, and the man doubled over. Shadlok brought the bow down on the man's arm and the sword went spinning from his grip. As quick as light, Shadlok snatched up the sword and ran the blade through the man's body.

William gasped at the spurt of blood that arced from the man's chest. He stumbled backwards, shocked and sickened, and barely noticed when Shadlok turned towards him and shouted, 'Behind you!'

William looked around but he was too late. Something hit him in the face. Sparks of light whirled through his head and his nose seemed to burst apart in a shower of hot blood. The next moment, the knife was knocked from his hand.

Acting purely on instinct, William threw himself forward, head down, and caught his opponent off guard. They fell to the ground and William hit out with his fists. Cold fingers, unbelievably strong, closed around his throat and squeezed tightly. William struggled harder, kicking out, flailing his fists, but the grip grew tighter.

The fingers suddenly loosened and the man slumped, a dead weight, on top of William.

William lay there for a few moments, dazed, and then he heaved the man's body aside and struggled to sit up. The man lay on his back and William saw him clearly for the first time. The deep-set eyes staring sightlessly into the winter sky were unnaturally green. The dead face was thin and sharply boned, the skin startlingly white. His hair spilled around his head like a pool of black water. There were two arrows in his side.

The dead creature was a fay.

Shadlok walked over to William, his face spattered with the creature's blood. He stared down at the body for a moment, tight-lipped. He held out a hand and helped William to his feet.

William dabbed at his throbbing nose with his sleeve, trying to wipe away the worst of the blood. It felt as if it had swollen to twice its size. The pain was making him dizzy.

Shadlok glanced at him. 'Unpleasant, but you will live.'

'Thanks,' William muttered thickly. There was blood in his mouth and he spat it out. He watched as

Shadlok retrieved his arrows and wiped the heads clean on the fay's tunic. He picked up his knife and handed it back to William.

'Keep this for now.'

William took the knife. His fingers shook so much he could barely hold it. 'They were fays,' he said, staring at the body on the ground. 'Why did they attack us?'

'They were warriors of the Dark King, my enemies.'

'But why attack you *now*?'

Shadlok did not look at him. 'I am sure they had their reasons.'

'Will there be more of them?' William asked.

'There are always more,' Shadlok said softly. 'Where is the hob?'

William pointed to the fallen branch. 'Over there. I told him to stay hidden.'

Shadlok walked across to the hob's hiding place and returned moments later with the hob following close behind.

Brother Walter looked horrified at the sight of William's face, but there was relief in the look, too. 'I thought you were dead.'

'No,' William said, blood bubbling from his nostrils. 'Still alive.'

'We are wasting time,' Shadlok said. 'Move quickly and stay watchful.' He set off at a run between the trees.

William lifted the hob onto his shoulders. He retrieved the pig-stick and hurried after Shadlok. Each step sent pain shooting through his head, but fear spurred him on and kept him going. All he could think of was getting back to the safety of the abbey.

They were within sight of the ditch and bank of the deer park when there was a sudden commotion in the undergrowth away to their right. His heart hammering with fright, William drew the knife from his belt and turned to face whatever was crashing through the trees towards them.

Two deer, panic-stricken, ran across the clearing. They shied away at the sight of William and leapt, stumbling and desperate, over the ditch and away over the top of the bank.

The hob wrapped his arms tightly around William's neck and whimpered beside his ear. Fear washed over William in cold waves as he stared into the tangled thickets and dark undergrowth, wondering what had frightened the deer. Were more fays following them through the forest?

Shadlok spun around to face William. 'Get back to

the abbey *now*. Run. Do not stop for anything.'

William paused just long enough to ask, 'What about you?'

'Just go!'

William did as he was told. Gripping the hob's good leg, he turned and ran for his life.

Chapter Twenty-One

William sprinted between the trees, leaping over ruts and potholes. His heart pounded as if it would beat its way out of his chest. The hob twisted his paws into William's hair and hung on tightly.

William reached the main track near the Boundary Oak. He stopped to catch his breath and leant against the tree for a few moments. In the distance, the abbey bell rang out for sext. The monks would be leaving whatever work they were busy with and filing into the church. By the time he reached the abbey, sext would be over, and they would be back about their tasks again. Suddenly, the abbey seemed to be the only safe place to be in a terrifying world.

Brother Walter gave several loud sniffs. 'Can you smell that?' he asked, patting William's head urgently. He sounded worried.

'Smell what?'

'Blood. Not yours. Someone else's.'

'Are you sure?' William asked uneasily.

'A *lot* of blood.'

William took the knife from his belt and gripped it firmly. Up ahead, the track curved northwards before branching in two. One way led to Crowfield, the other to Yagleah. They were almost within sight of the abbey now.

William walked quickly, the knife ready in his hand. He peered between the trees, alert for the slightest sign of danger. 'Can you see anything?' he asked.

'No, but I can still smell blood.'

They rounded the bend in the track near the abbey bridge. William was appalled by the sight that met his eyes.

The bodies of animals and birds hung from the branches of trees and bushes on either side of the track, hung up by tails or limbs or wings, blood dripping from slit throats. He recognised one of the abbey's two young pigs. His throat thickened as he wondered what had happened to Mary Magdalene. Beside the pig hung a doe, her wide brown eyes fixed and staring in death.

William gazed at the scene of carnage, his body rigid with horror. The hob clung to his neck. He lifted the creature down from his shoulders. 'Stay there,' he said, his voice hoarse.

One by one, William took the animals and birds down from the branches and laid them on the grass beside the track. The deer and the pig were heavy and he had to let them drop to the ground by themselves. Their bodies were still warm. They could not have been dead for long.

For a few moments, he held the small bodies of a wren and a robin in his hands. Hot tears filled his eyes as he stroked their soft feathers with his thumbs. He was sickened by the pointless cruelty of their deaths. He laid them on the grass by the body of a fox cub.

William wiped his eyes on a corner of his sleeve and looked around for the hob. Brother Walter, looking small and unhappy, limped over to him. His fur stood in untidy tufts, and his tail dragged along the ground behind him as if the effort of lifting it was simply too much. William lifted him up and put him on his shoulders. They walked the last of the way back to the abbey in heavy-hearted silence. William's hands and the front of his tunic were smeared with blood but he barely noticed.

Burning anger filled William's chest until he thought it would burst. He knew without the slightest doubt that the massacre was the work of the Dark King's creatures. Was it meant as a threat to Shadlok, a promise of what they were prepared to do to him if he crossed them? William had never hated anyone in his life before, but as he walked over the bridge to the abbey gatehouse, hatred for the fay king raged inside him. Later, if he could slip away from the abbey for a while, he would go back to Foxwist and bury the bodies. There was nothing else he could do for them.

Chapter Twenty-Two

Brother Snail was in his workshop, stirring a pot over the fire. His smile of welcome turned to a gasp of shock at the sight of William, blood-stained and battered, standing in the doorway.

'Will! What in the name of God has happened to you?' He hurried over and took William by the arm and led him over to a stool.

'It looks worse than it is. Most of the blood's not mine,' William said.

'Whose is it?' The monk examined William's nose. He ran a finger gently over his cheek. 'Whose blood is it, Will?'

'It belongs to animals we found slaughtered in the wood, not far from the abbey.'

Brother Snail stared at him in astonishment for a moment. 'What animals?'

'Foxes, birds, a deer. One of the abbey pigs. Other

creatures,' William said softly, his throat thickening again as he thought of the row of bodies on the grass, still warm as they lay there in their own blood.

'I see,' the monk said evenly. He fetched a bowl of water, some linen rags and a small jar of salve and set them down on the table. He dipped a rag into the water. 'Let's get you cleaned up, and then you can tell me what's been going on.'

William gasped as the cold cloth touched his skin. Brother Snail wiped the blood away, gently and skilfully. He rinsed the cloth and blood swirled in the water.

'There is a cut across your nose, and a deep one on your cheek. They will leave scars. Hold this in place,' he said, wringing the cloth out and laying it across William's face. 'It will help the swelling to go down.' He stepped back and stood, hands tucked into the sleeves of his habit, to look sideways at William. 'Now, how did this happen? Start at the beginning and leave nothing out.'

William told him everything, from the hob's arrival in the swineherd's hut and the visit to Dame Alys, to finding the bodies by the track. Brother Snail listened intently, his eyes bright with anger, his lips clamped tightly shut.

'To think we sent you to the hut to keep you safe,' the monk said when William had finished his story. He took the cloth from William's face and picked up the jar of woundwort salve. He scooped a little out with his fingertips and gently smeared it across William's cheeks and nose. The salve stung for a couple of moments, making William's eyes water.

'Why did the Dark King's warriors kill those animals, do you think?' the monk asked.

'A warning, maybe. They don't want Shadlok and Master Bone to find the angel.'

'And you say the Dark King is somehow to blame for Jacobus Bone's leprosy?' Brother Snail said, looking down at William, a worried look on his thin face.

'He wanted to punish Master Bone for being a great musician, and for being the favourite of the Seelie queen,' William said. It was an effort to talk without hurting his face. He had to say each word slowly, forming the sound with care.

'Very effective,' Snail said grimly, 'and deeply evil and malicious, especially if Master Bone really is immortal.'

'He is, according to Brother Walter. The hob knows all about it.'

Brother Snail frowned and looked around. 'Where *is* the hob?'

'Outside the hut. He's keeping watch in case any fays have followed us back here.'

'This is a bad business, Will.' Brother Snail sighed heavily and walked to the door. His movements were slow and stiff this morning. He pulled up the hood of his cowl and took his cloak from a peg by the door. He eased it around his bowed shoulders. 'I have to tell the prior what has happened. Come with me, but say nothing about the Dark King or Master Bone's part in all this. One last thing, Will, you say you know where the angel is buried?'

'I think the monks buried it in the Whistling Hollow.'

Brother Snail nodded slowly as he considered this. 'I think you could very well be right.'

'Should I tell Master Bone and Shadlok where the grave is?' William asked.

The monk was quiet for a moment. 'Do you have any idea why they want to find it?'

'The hob thinks they want to use the bones for a magic spell, to cure Master Bone's leprosy.'

'Does he now?' Snail raised his eyebrows.

'Would it harm to let them use a bone or two?'

William said. 'The angel doesn't need them.'

'I honestly don't know,' Snail said. He opened the door and stared out at the bleak winter's day. It was a few moments before he spoke again. 'There is nothing to say the bones are still there, Will. The ground in the Hollow is damp. Perhaps they've rotted away over the last hundred years.'

'But if we can find them, would it be so wrong to let Master Bone use one for his cure?' William asked. He did not particularly like Jacobus Bone but he felt a deep pity for the man. To be condemned to an unending life of suffering and loneliness was a terrible thing. But it was more than that; if he helped Master Bone, then he would be fighting back against the Dark King and his fays. He wanted some small revenge for what they had done to the animals.

'We have to ask ourselves if the angel would have wanted to help Master Bone,' Snail said slowly. 'If the answer is yes, then we should tell him where the grave is.'

William said nothing. How could anyone possibly guess what thoughts went through an angel's mind?

'All we know for sure is that he gave his own life to save the life of a lowly hob. I think that tells us what we need to know,' the monk said with a fleeting smile.

'So we're going to tell Master Bone where the grave is?'

The monk nodded and crossed himself, fingers touching forehead, chest and either shoulder. His face was pale and drawn. 'God forgive me if I am making the wrong choice, Will, but yes, we are.'

'Prior Ardo would probably burn us at the stake for allowing the angel's grave to be disturbed,' William said, coming to stand beside Brother Snail, 'and for letting such holy bones be used for magic.'

The monk rubbed his hands together to ease the ache in his fingers. His face was pinched with pain. 'That is why we must keep this matter to ourselves, Will. Nobody at Crowfield must ever find out about this.'

William nodded his heartfelt agreement. The Dark King's anger would be as pale as the moon at midday compared to the prior's wrath if he discovered what they had done. Not to mention what God might have to say about all this when they stood before Him on Judgement Day.

William followed the monk out into the cold afternoon and closed the hut door behind him. The chilly breeze ruffled his hair and made his broken nose ache. There was no sign of the hob. William hoped he had found somewhere warm and safe to keep watch from.

'I will speak to Master Bone,' the monk said, tucking his hands into the sleeves of his habit. 'Go back to your work and keep your head down, Will. This doesn't concern you any longer.'

William started to protest but Brother Snail shook his head. There was a warning gleam in his eyes.

'No, Will, no arguments. You could have died today. Whatever Master Bone and Shadlok do from now on will not involve you in any way, do you understand? The Dark King is *their* enemy, not yours. Don't be so quick to pick a fight with a foe you cannot hope to defeat.'

There was a sudden commotion as two pigs, followed closely by Shadlok, emerged from the woods across the river. One of the pigs charged around, ears flapping, squealing with excitement. The other pig, William was delighted to see, was Mary Magdalene. She crossed the flood meadow to the abbey bridge at a sedate trot.

'Go and open the gate, Will,' Brother Snail said, smiling broadly.

William raced away, jumping over rows of cabbages and skidding on the gravel path. When he reached the gatehouse, he found that Brother Stephen had beaten him to it and was kneeling on the bridge, hugging Mary Magdalene. The pig grunted softly and seemed to be just as pleased to see the monk as he was to see her. Shadlok herded the other pig towards the gate.

William opened the wicker gate of the pigpen. The young pig, sensing defeat, ran across the yard and into the pen without any further fuss. Mary Magdalene followed a few moments later and flopped down in the straw.

Brother Stephen wiped his nose on his sleeve. His eyes gleamed with tears. He stood by the pen, gazing fondly down at the old sow. He glanced at William and frowned at the sight of his broken nose.

'What happened to you, boy? Did you run into trouble in the woods? And where is the other pig?'

'We were attacked by . . . outlaws. Shadlok came to our rescue.' Broadly speaking, it was true. 'The other pig is dead.'

'Does the prior know about this?'

'Brother Snail has gone to tell him.'

Brother Stephen nodded. 'Very well. Seeing as you're here, you can make yourself useful. An apple tree has come down at the far end of the orchard. Fetch the axe and cut it up, and put the logs to one side in the woodshed.'

Apple wood, William knew, burned with a pleasant smell. It was one of the few small indulgences the monks enjoyed, a fire of apple wood in the warming room on the cold dark days around Christmastide.

William took the large wood axe from where it hung on the wall of the small barn and set off to the orchard. The woundwort salve had eased the pain of his broken nose and cleared his head. He looked up at the grey winter sky and breathed in slowly and deeply. In a day or two, Master Bone and Shadlok would be on their way and his days would settle back into their familiar routine. It was not the life he would have chosen for himself, but at least it would be filled with commonplace things, and not fays and their danger-ous magic. After the events of the last few days, he would happily settle for that.

'Did you speak to the prior?' William asked when he saw Brother Snail in the yard a short time later. He was pushing a handcart full of apple logs to the wood-shed and stopped for a few minutes to talk to the monk.

Brother Snail nodded. 'I told him you were set upon by outlaws, and that Master Bone's servant came to your aid.'

'It's a strange outlaw who kills birds and animals and hangs them from trees,' William said, frowning at the memory.

'The prior thinks so too,' Brother Snail said. 'Nevertheless, he means to send word to Sir Robert at Weforde to warn him that outlaws are attacking people in Foxwist. And he has no intention of sending you back to the swineherd's hut.'

William was relieved to hear this.

'I have also told Shadlok where the grave is,' the monk lowering his voice and glancing around to make sure they were not being overheard. His eyes were troubled, as if even now, he was still not sure he had done the right thing. 'It is up to him what he does next, if he decides to go to the Hollow or not.'

'He'll go,' William said with complete certainty.

'Well, he will have to go soon,' Brother Snail said, 'because the prior has asked Master Bone to leave the abbey. And God forgive me for being so uncharitable, Will, but I'll be heartily glad to see him go.'

Chapter Twenty-Three

Soon after dinner, Brother Martin set off across the bridge with the handcart. He returned a short time later with the dead pig. It lay on the cart, head lolling over the side. The monk spotted William chopping the apple logs into smaller pieces outside the woodshed.

'Hoi! You! We have work to do. Get the trestle table and pig-frame set up in the yard.'

William set off across the yard to do as he was told. Cutting the pig into joints, ready for salting, would take the rest of the afternoon but William did not mind; it would keep him busy and give him no time to worry about the dark fay world beyond the abbey gates.

Brother Martin sent William to fetch a pile of straw from the barn. They laid the pig on top of it and the monk set light to the straw. When the pig's bristles had burned away, Brother Martin heaved the carcass up and hung it from the lintel of the smokehouse doorway, from hooks through the hind leg hocks. William stood well back as the monk slit the animal from belly to throat and hauled out the innards.

'Hang 'em up to dry,' Brother Martin ordered, 'and put the loose fat into that bucket.'

William did as he was told, working quickly to try and keep up with the swiping blade of Brother Martin's knife.

With worrying skill, the monk split the pig in half with a small axe. Off came the hocks, the head and the hams. He slapped each joint down on the trestle table William had set up nearby, until the pig was no more than various sized lumps of pink flesh. Its head lay at one end of the table, eyes half closed, mouth seemingly curved in a smile.

'Get them guts cleaned,' Brother Martin ordered, pointing to the knobbly ropes of intestines hanging from the wooden drying frame beside the table.

It was a smelly, horrible job and William gagged several times as he squeezed the pig's last meal out onto the cobbles. He put the guts into a pail of water and swirled the slimy mess around with a stick to wash them. Brother Martin would pack lengths of the innards with chopped-up bits of fat and the scrapings from the bones, along with herbs and barley and oats, to make puddings. Normally he would have added the blood from the slaughtered animal to the mixture, but that had soaked away into the earth in Foxwist Wood.

'Bloody wasteful,' the monk snarled, glaring at William as if he was to blame for the loss of the blood. He flicked a contemptuous hand at the innards in the pail. 'Puddings as pale as bloody maggots and mealy with it, this lot'll be. Should be stiff with good black blood.' He spat on the cobbles and wiped the blade of his knife on the front of his filthy apron. He turned on his heel and walked off to the kitchen.

William finished cleaning the intestines, rinsed them in the greasy water and hung them to dry on the frame. As soon as Brother Martin prepared the salt water to soak the pork in, William would carry the meat into the kitchen and pack it into the pickle barrels. In a few days' time, when the meat was wrinkly-pale and salted to the monk's satisfaction, it would be hung in the smokehouse until it was as dark and hard as leather, or stored in small barrels of brine, to be used over the coming winter months.

William hauled up a bucket of water from the well and washed his hands, rubbing them together hard to try and get rid of the smell of the dead pig. The freezing water numbed his fingers. They would be painful later, when they warmed up and the feeling slowly returned.

At first, William did not take any notice of the raised voices coming from somewhere inside the abbey, but the voices became more insistent. He straightened up and dried his hands on his tunic. *What now?* he thought wearily.

The yard door of the kitchen opened and a frightened-looking Peter peered out.

'Will!' he called, his voice sharp with anguish. 'Come quickly!'

For a moment, William thought Abbot Simon must have died.

'It's Brother Snail,' Peter twisted his fingers together against his chest. 'I think he is dead.'

For several moments, William could not move. It felt as if the bones had been drawn from his legs. He began to shake.

'Brother Snail?' he whispered. Pain seared through his chest, making it difficult to breathe.

Then he was running across the yard. He pushed Peter aside and collided with Brother Martin in the kitchen. He ignored the monk's angry yell and ran out into the cloister alley. Peter followed close behind. William stopped by the archway leading into the cloister garth.

A small dark bundle lay across one of the newly dug herb beds. Brother Gabriel and Prior Ardo knelt beside it, shocked expressions on their faces.

William walked slowly forward. His whole body was numb with shock and disbelief. He sank to his knees on the path. Gravel bit into his knees, but he barely noticed.

Brother Gabriel rolled Snail onto his side, the plump hands gently cradling the stricken monk's head.

'Is he dead?' the prior asked, his voice sounding strained, his face grey with shock.

Brother Gabriel held a hand close to Brother Snail's mouth, and then lowered his head to listen to Snail's chest.

'I think so.'

'No,' William said desperately. 'He can't be.' He touched the side of the monk's neck, as Snail had once shown him how to do. There seemed to be a faint pulse. William's hands were trembling so much he could not be sure if he had really felt it. Taking several deep, steadying breaths, he tried again.

'He's still alive,' he said, hope bursting into life inside him. 'Feel here, on his neck.'

Frowning, Brother Gabriel did so. He glanced up at the prior. 'The boy is right. There is a pulse, very weak, but it *is* there.'

The prior looked around. By now, all the monks were gathered around, watching anxiously.

'We need to get him off the cold ground. Brother Stephen, and you, Peter, lift him up and carry him to the infirmary. Be quick, now.'

Between them, the lay brother and the monk carried Snail across the garth and into the cloister alley. Prior Ardo turned to face the remaining monks.

'Go about your work. There is nothing you can do for our brother now except pray for him.'

Reluctantly, the monks dispersed and went back to whatever tasks they were supposed to be doing.

'You, too, boy,' the prior said, glancing down at William. His expression softened for a moment. 'He is in God's hands now.'

William watched the small procession make its way around to the passageway beside the chapter house. He thought of the small infirmary, set well away from the abbey buildings and as lonely as a boat on a pond, a short distance beyond the monks' graveyard. He decided to take a basket of firewood there straight away, a little of the precious apple wood. The prior had told him to get on with his work, and that was one of his tasks. At least that way, he would be able to see for himself that Brother Snail had been made as comfortable as possible.

William took the basket from beside the fireplace in the kitchen and ran across the yard to the wood-shed. He was piling logs and branches into it when a shadow fell across the woodpile. He looked over his shoulder and saw Shadlok standing in the hut doorway.

'The monk told us where to find the angel's grave.'

'I know,' William said impatiently. He did not care about the angel or Master Bone. The only person who mattered at that moment was Brother Snail.

'Master Bone and I will leave tomorrow,' Shadlok said, 'soon after noon.'

William frowned. 'Do what you want, it's none of my concern.'

'We will go to the Hollow,' the fay continued as if William had not spoken. 'The angel must be taken from its grave before the Dark King's followers find us and try to stop us.'

So the hob was right, William thought with a shiver;

Shadlok and Master Bone wanted the angel's bones for a healing spell.

'Can't you just take one bone and leave the rest of the angel's remains in peace?' William asked, straightening up.

A flicker of surprise crossed the fay's sharp features. 'That is not possible.'

'Why not?'

'You will see for yourself tomorrow.'

William frowned. 'What do you mean?'

'You are coming with us to the Hollow.'

William stared at him in disbelief. 'Me?'

Shadlok said nothing.

'No,' William said, shaking his head. 'No, I won't. And you can't make me.'

'Oh, I think you will,' Shadlok said, his voice as soft as the whisper of a blade through the air, 'if you want the monk to wake again.'

As the meaning of the fay's words slowly dawned on him, cold rage surged through William's body.

'What have you done to him?' His hands clenched into fists and he took a step towards Shadlok. 'If he dies, I will kill you.'

The fay smiled thinly. 'You care deeply for your friend. It is your weakness, human, and it makes you vulnerable. You will help us tomorrow because if you do not, then the monk *will* die.'

'You bastard!' William spat, his face close to Shadlok's.

Shadlok's eyes narrowed. 'Tomorrow at midday, be waiting for us by the gatehouse. Live or die, the monk's fate is in your hands.'

'Prior Ardo will never agree to let me go with you,' William said.

'He will.' Without another word, Shadlok turned and walked away across the yard.

Angry tears filled William's eyes. He grabbed the axe from the chopping block and swung it blindly at a pile of logs. Bits of wood flew up. One piece hit him on his injured cheek and the sting of pain made him angrier still. He hacked at the logs and let his rage and frustration spill out. He hated Shadlok for using Brother Snail as a weapon to force him to dig up the grave; he hated the fay for being prepared to harm one of the few truly good people William had ever known.

At last, his fury spent, William sat on the floor, his back against the shed wall. He folded his arms across his up-drawn knees and rested his head on the coarse wool of his sleeve. A great weariness settled over him. His broken nose throbbed painfully and he felt sick.

He had no choice but to go to the Whistling Hollow tomorrow. Brother Snail's life depended on it. And he knew, with a dreadful certainty, that creatures of the Dark King would be in the woods, waiting for them.

For a moment, self-pity weakened him and tears stung his eyes. To think he had felt sorry for Jacobus Bone! To think he and Snail had imagined they were doing the right thing in trying to help him find a cure for his leprosy. If they had kept the location of the grave secret, then the monk would not be lying close to death in the infirmary, and William would not be facing an uncertain and possibly very short future at the hands of the Dark King's fays. One small act of compassion could well have cost them both their lives.

Chapter Twenty-Four

The infirmary stood between the monks' burial ground and the sheep pasture. Brother Snail had once told William that it was easier to stop sickness from spreading if patients could be kept isolated. It was built of timber and thatch, and if it had not been for the small shuttered windows set high up in the walls, it could easily have been mistaken for a barn.

William carried the basket of firewood into the small building. Shafts of grey winter light streaked down through the stale and dusty air from the gaps around the edges of the shutters. There were four beds in the single room, plain wooden frames with straw mattresses. At the far end of the room there was a wooden altar, covered with a white linen cloth. A simple iron crucifix was nailed to the wall above it. There were brackets around the walls for rushlights.

Two iron braziers were the only source of heating in the infirmary, as far as William could see.

Brother Gabriel was making a bed up for Snail from the bundle of blankets he had hurriedly grabbed from the bedding cupboard outside the monks' dormitory. William dragged one of the braziers closer to the monk's bed and got a fire going.

Peter and Brother Stephen lowered Snail onto the bed, rolling him onto his side. Brother Gabriel pulled the blankets up to cover him. Only his face and one hand showed.

Brother Odo, elderly and deaf, was chosen to stay with Brother Snail. He was too old to be useful around the abbey and its fields, but he still had his most of his wits and could be trusted to watch over the unconscious monk.

'Fetch me if there is any change in our brother's condition,' Prior Ardo said loudly, forming the words with exaggerated care. Brother Odo watched the prior's lips and nodded.

The prior, Brother Stephen and Brother Gabriel left the dormitory, their mouths moving in silent prayer, their heads bowed. They had no idea what was wrong with Brother Snail and William had no intention of telling them. If he crossed Shadlok, then the fay would kill the monk for sure.

Brother Odo took no notice of William, but went to pray at the altar. His knees were stiff and he could no longer kneel, so he sat on a stool, eyes fixed on the cross on the wall, his hands loosely clasped together.

William stood beside Snail's bed for a few minutes, staring down at the monk's pale face. He felt as if his heart was breaking into small pieces. What was the point of caring for people if all they did was leave you? His brother Hugh had left home without a backward glance, and the rest of his family had gone to another place without him. And now Brother Snail was hidden away somewhere inside the small crippled body, out of reach.

He heard a soft rustling in the straw by his feet, and glanced down to see the hob crawl out from under the bed.

'Is the snail brother dying?' the hob asked. His small face was pinched with anxiety.

'Shadlok has put him under a spell of some kind,' William said softly.

The hob climbed onto the bed and sat beside Brother Snail. He lifted one of the monk's eyelids. 'That is very bad. Why did he do it?'

'To make sure I'll help him dig up the angel's grave

tomorrow. If I don't, he will let Brother Snail die.'

Brother Walter's eyes widened in surprise. 'You told him where it is?'

'Brother Snail did, and this was the thanks he got,' William said bitterly.

The hob settled himself against Brother Snail's back. His tail curled across the monk's neck, the tufted end tucked beneath Snail's cheek. 'I will stay with him.'

William nodded. 'Good. Look after him. I will bring you some food later. Take care around Brother Odo, he's old and deaf but his eyes and wits are sharp enough.'

'He will not see me, he does not have the Sight,' the hob said.

William looked at him suspiciously. 'How do you know that?'

'He almost sat on me in the place where the brother men go to sing to their god. The place with the stone people.'

'You were in the church?' William asked, not pleased to hear this. 'What were you doing there?'

The hob lifted one shoulder in a shrug. 'Just looking at the stone plants and birds and people.'

'And he nearly sat on you?'

The hob nodded. 'The other brother men stand up to sing, or they kneel down. That one sits down.' He paused for a moment and frowned over at Brother Odo's back. 'Except I was already sitting on the seat. I only just moved in time. But he did not see me.'

'I told you not to wander around the abbey,' William said, exasperated by the hob's indifference to the danger he was putting himself in. 'I have work to do in the kitchen, but we'll talk about this later.'

The hob sniffed and pulled the edge of the blanket around his shoulders. William added another couple of logs to the brazier and left the infirmary.

The last grey glow of daylight faded in the western sky. The fields and woods around the abbey were peaceful and still in the freezing dusk, apart from the distant cawing of crows settling to roost for the night. William shivered as he hurried through the graveyard, heading for the passageway to the cloister. The bell for vespers rang out, clear and sharp, a little later than usual, though that was hardly surprising after the events of the day.

At least Brother Snail was safe enough for the moment, William thought, and the hob would watch over him. For now, that was all that mattered.

Chapter Twenty-Five

As he stood shivering by the well soon after dawn the following morning, William looked up at the clouds building up in the sky to the north. There would be snow before nightfall.

William was preoccupied as he went about his morning chores. He fetched water, carried firewood, took food to Brother Odo and the hob in the infirmary and helped Peter to carry turnips from the small shed at the far end of the garden to the kitchen. Time and again, his thoughts turned to what lay ahead, to the walk through the forest to the Hollow. When they got there, how would they find the grave? And what if the monks had buried the angel deep in the earth?

No, he told himself, they wouldn't have. They had dug the grave at night, in a snowstorm, and they had been in a hurry. The grave would be shallow.

On his way to fetch a basket of kindling from the

woodshed, he saw Shadlok sharpening the blade of his sword on the big circular whetstone in the carpentry shed. The fay glanced up at him but said nothing. William paused in the doorway, listening to the rasp of metal on stone.

'What if we don't find the . . . what we're looking for?' William asked, glancing around, even though he knew there was nobody about. The monks were all in the church for mass.

Shadlok lifted the sword blade from the whetstone and examined the cutting edge. 'We will find it.'

'We might not,' William persisted. 'There might be nothing left.'

Shadlok's eyes narrowed. There was a warning note in his voice. 'I said, we will find it.'

William watched as Shadlok polished the blade with a rag. The metal gleamed, sharp and deadly.

'Why do you want me there with you?' William asked. It was something that had been troubling him. The fay was strong enough to dig out the grave in half the time it would take William. Shadlok did not *need* his help.

The cold blue eyes glanced at him briefly. 'I have my reasons.'

'Do you ever give a straight answer to a question?'

William asked, exasperated.

'Sometimes.' Shadlok held the sword up and turned it slowly. It glinted in the light and William saw an interlaced pattern welded into the blade.

William waited to see if the fay had anything else to say, but he didn't.

'Just don't forget your promise not to harm Brother Snail,' William said.

'I did not promise,' Shadlok said, sheathing the sword. As he brushed past William, he added, 'I do not make promises to humans.'

William watched him walk away across the yard with deep dislike. Shadlok was a Seelie fay, a creature of the light, but as far as William could see, he was no better than the Dark King.

William fetched a shovel from the barn. Brother Stephen kept all the abbey's tools clean and well cared for, so the shovel was good and solid, with a sharp iron blade. He let himself out through the wicket gate and hid it in the reeds beside the bridge. It would be safe there until he retrieved it on his way to the Hollow.

When the bells for sext clanged out at noon, William made his way to the gatehouse to wait for Master Bone and Shadlok. He wondered what excuse

Master Bone had given for wanting William to leave the abbey with him. What if the prior refused to let William go? There was a flutter of panic in William's chest. Would Shadlok just let Brother Snail die?

William paced back and forth as he tried to keep warm. A chilly breeze played chase with dead leaves and bits of straw across the yard. It was not a day to be standing around, and even the hens had chosen to stay indoors. At last, Shadlok and Master Bone walked around the corner of the west range, accompanied by Prior Ardo and, at a safe distance, Brother Gabriel.

Brother Stephen led three horses out of the stable and waited while Shadlok helped his master to climb up into the saddle. The third horse was Matilda, the abbey's mare. She carried bundles and bags of Master Bone's possessions. The rest of his things would be sent for later.

'Here, boy!' the prior called, beckoning William over. 'Lead the mare to Sir Robert's house at Weforde for Master Bone. You can stay there tonight, and Shadlok will see you get back safely in the morning.'

William took the mare's reins. Dread was like a lead weight in the pit of his stomach. He glanced at Shadlok, but the fay's face was expressionless.

The prior did not look happy with the arrangement,

but William suspected he had been paid well for his trouble. He turned to Master Bone and added, 'I sent our lay brother Peter to Yagleah this morning, to warn them that outlaws were at large in Foxwist again. They'll have taken word to Sir Robert by now and he'll have sent his men into the forest to hunt for them. Your passage to Weforde should be safe enough, God willing.'

'Thank you for your kindness,' Master Bone said, his voice muffled behind the mask. He bowed his head slowly to the prior. It was hard to tell if he was being sarcastic or not. A flush rose to Prior Ardo's sallow cheeks and he looked uncomfortable. He must have been aware of how thinly spread his hospitality had been.

'Travel safely, and God protect you,' the prior said stiffly.

Shadlok turned his horse's head and set off towards the gatehouse. Master Bone followed. William gave Matilda's reins a gentle tug and she ambled after him. The prior caught hold of William's arm and with a wary glance at Master Bone, whispered, 'Keep your distance from them, boy, as much as possible. Do not touch Master Bone's possessions any more than you have to, and do not let him breathe on you.'

'I'll try not to,' William said. At least he and the prior were in agreement about that.

The prior nodded. 'We will pray for you.'

The gates were closed and barred behind them before they were halfway across the bridge. William retrieved the shovel and wedged it between two bags on the mare's back.

William wore every bit of clothing he owned, as well as a pair of coarse woollen mittens he had borrowed from Peter, but he was still cold. His nose hurt more today than it had yesterday and he knew his face was mottled with bruises, because Peter had told him so. He also knew a broken nose was likely to be the least of his problems by the end of the day. I'll be lucky if I still *have* a nose, he thought, or anything else, come to that.

Jacobus Bone was hunched forward in his saddle, the stumps of his hands resting on the pommel. There was an air of utter weariness about him and William felt a stir of pity for the man. It would take a harder heart than William's to begrudge Master Bone his cure.

Shadlok looked relaxed as he rode along. One hand rested lightly on his thigh and his shoulders were back. If he was worried about what lay ahead, it did not show.

They passed the sad huddle of dead animals and birds. Feathers and fur were damp and bedraggled, eyes clouded with death. William's mouth hardened into a straight line as he stared at the bodies. If he survived what was to follow, he would come back and bury them.

They reached the Boundary Oak. Up ahead, William could see the rag-hung trees and bushes near the Hollow and his stomach tightened with fear. There was no escape now and the enormity of what he was about to do left him breathless.

'Frightened, William?' Jacobus asked, his thin voice just a hoarse rasp.

'A little,' William admitted.

'We have asked a great deal of you today, and for that I am truly sorry,' Jacobus continued, 'but you will be rewarded for your help. What is it you would most like to have? I am a wealthy man and I will grant you whatever you ask, if it is in my power to do so.'

'There is one thing I want,' William said.

'Name it and it will be yours.'

'I want Brother Snail to wake up from whatever spell *he* put him under,' William said, jerking his head towards Shadlok. The fay glanced over his shoulder, a look of surprise on his face.

Master Bone was silent for a moment. 'And that is all you want?'

'Yes.'

Jacobus nodded slowly. William had the feeling that Master Bone was pleased by his answer.

'We chose well, my old friend,' Jacobus said softly, leaning towards Shadlok.

'So it would seem,' Shadlok replied, his tone giving nothing away.

'There is no doubt about it. Only one pure in heart and gifted with the Sight will be able to complete the task, you know that,' Jacobus went on, gently insistent. William had to listen hard to catch the whispered words. 'This boy is both. He *must* be the one.'

'We will find out soon enough.' Shadlok stared straight ahead.

What did Jacobus mean, he was *the one*? William wondered. It seemed they were not merely bringing him along to help dig out the grave but had chosen him for some other task. He didn't like the sound of that at all.

'The horses will not be able to get through the under-growth,' Shadlok said, dismounting. 'We will leave them over there, out of sight.' He nodded to the scrub on the far side of the track, away from the Hollow.

William led Matilda between the trees and tied her reins securely to a hazel sapling. If he did not return to the abbey, for whatever reason, the monks would not have too much trouble finding her. They would not be able to see her but if she was hungry enough, they would certainly hear her.

Shadlok helped Jacobus to dismount and then led their horses into the wood. William unpacked the shovel and walked back to the track to wait for them.

'Are the Dark King's warriors following us?' he asked, shivering inside his woollen tunic and jacket. His fingers inside the mittens were numb with cold.

'No,' Shadlok said, 'though it will only be a matter of time before they find us. Do you still have the knife I gave you, human?'

William nodded and lifted aside the front of his jacket, to show the knife tucked into his belt.

'Good. Now, lead the way.'

William walked over to the edge of the track. Taking a deep breath, he put his arms up to protect his face and forced his way between the holly bushes. The wood was more overgrown than he remembered. Thorns snagged his clothing and scratched his face and neck. Holly branches caught in his hair and trailing ivy stems wrapped around his ankles and tried to trip him up. He pushed branches aside with the shovel and grunted with the effort of pulling free from vicious ropes of bramble, whose huge thorns could easily rip flesh from bone.

The ground sloped gradually downhill and he saw the dark bulk of the yew tree a little way ahead. They were almost there. Only another twenty paces or so and they would reach the clearing around the pool.

And then he heard it, a soft, low whistle. He froze. It came again and his blood turned to ice. Surely no living creature could make that unearthly sound? He looked over his shoulder at Shadlok. The fay's expression was grim, his eyes wide and fierce.

'Keep moving,' Shadlok said.

William pushed on through the undergrowth. His shoulders were hunched up to his ears as he tried to block out the whistling. He could not work out where it was coming from; one moment it seemed to be up ahead, the next it was right beside him. Sweat ran down between his shoulder blades, quickly cooling on his chilled body. He edged his way around the yew and was relieved to see the steely glint of the pool through the tangled thicket ahead of him. The whistling faded into a sibilant hiss that made the hairs on the back of his neck stand on end. It rose and fell, like something breathing.

Shadlok's knuckles dug William in the back, forcing him to keep walking.

The sound died away on a long sigh. The silence that followed made William's skin crawl; there was nothing to see or hear, but the sense of being watched was overwhelming.

Faint ripples spread across the dark surface of the pool as water from the spring trickled into it. Shadows gathered in the undergrowth and the grey afternoon light leached away what little colour there might have been in the woodland around the clearing.

William reached the hazel tree and looked around. He hugged the shovel to his chest and shivered, as much from fear as cold. 'Where do we start digging?'

The Hollow was as large as the monks' graveyard at the abbey. How were they supposed to find one unmarked grave here? It could take days, and they might only have minutes.

Shadlok frowned as he gazed around. For once, William noticed with a trace of satisfaction, he did not look so sure of himself. He pointed to a level patch of ground near the hazel tree. 'Start there.'

William scraped aside the dead leaves, then swung the shovel into the earth and began to dig.

For a while, the only sound in the Hollow was the ring of metal on stone as William hacked away at the hard ground.

Shadlok kept watch for unwelcome visitors, prowling around the edge of the clearing, sword in hand. Jacobus Bone sat on a fallen tree, a silent, hunched figure, watching William as he worked.

The roots of the hazel tree were a twisted tangle in the earth. It was impossible to dig through them. William leant on the handle of the shovel for a few moments to rest his aching shoulder muscles. The tree was old, its trunk as broad as a man's neck and the mossy bark deeply scored. It must have been growing here when the angel was buried, or the monk would not have drawn the hazelnut as a clue. The grave had to be close by, but not *this* close to the roots.

'Why have you stopped?' Shadlok called.

'The grave can't be here. There are too many roots.'

The fay made an impatient noise and sprinted lightly down the slope to stand beside him. 'Where, then?'

William turned on him angrily. 'I don't know! I wasn't here when they buried the body, I didn't draw the pictures on the book page. None of this has anything to do with me. I *don't know!*'

Shadlok looked startled by his outburst. He sheathed his sword and took the shovel from William. He walked slowly around the clearing, jabbing at the ground every few paces. There was an intent look on his face. A short distance from the pool, just before the ground sloped uphill, he stopped.

'Here,' he said, holding the shovel out to William. 'Dig here.'

A sudden breeze stirred the branches of the trees around the clearing. William caught a movement out of the corner of his eye. A grey mist was rising up from the surface of the pool. It coiled between the dead reeds and up through the branches of the hazel tree. The whistling started again, like the single note from a pipe. The sound seemed to get inside William's head.

'Dig!' Shadlok said sharply, pushing the shovel into William's shaking hands.

The earth was just soft and damp enough for the shovel blade to cut through without too much back-breaking effort. Nevertheless, it was still hard work. William hacked and scraped as fast as he could, fear making his movements clumsy. He stopped just long enough to pull off his hood, jacket and the thick woollen mittens. He threw them aside and rolled up the sleeves of his tunic.

Shadlok moved to stand between William and the pool. The mist spread out across the clearing, creeping purposefully towards William. The whistling turned to furious, ear-splitting shrieks that made him flinch with pain. Shadlok stood his ground, saying something in a low voice, words that William did not understand. He could feel their power, though, and knew Shadlok was battling the misty presence in the clearing with magic. The mist coiled and seethed and radiated malevolence, but came no closer to the grave.

The hole beneath William's feet was growing bigger by the minute. There were no roots to hinder him, just stones and black earth. Sweat ran into his eyes. He wiped it away with his sleeve. His broken nose throbbed with pain and his back and shoulders ached. Something touched his face and he glanced up. A few snowflakes, as soft as lambswool, drifted idly down between the lattice of branches overhead. The daylight was starting to fade.

There was a muttered curse from Shadlok and William was alarmed to see the fay take a few steps backwards. The mist was gaining strength.

'Quickly, human. We are running out of time,' Shadlok said urgently.

On the far side of the clearing, Jacobus struggled to his feet and even at this distance, William could hear the man's ragged and gasping breath as he watched what was happening.

Terrified, William shovelled the earth from the bottom of the hole as hard and fast as he could. Something pale caught his eye and he crouched down to take a closer look.

It was a piece of white cloth. William's hand shook as he pulled at it. More of the material unravelled and came free. It was as white as goose down and far too clean for something that had been in the earth for a hundred years. William sat back on his heels and stared at the cloth uneasily. There was something very odd about this.

'I think I've found it,' he called, his voice unsteady.

Jacobus took a couple of faltering steps forward, his whole body quivering with excitement. Shadlok pushed past William and knelt down to scrape the loose earth aside, uncovering more of the white material.

William gasped as Shadlok pulled aside a fold of fabric to reveal a hand. A deathly pale, long-fingered hand, perfect and whole.

'I . . . I don't understand . . .' William stammered,

turning to Shadlok. 'I thought there would be just bones.'

The fay's face showed no surprise. There was not enough room in the hole for two people, so William scrambled out and stood shivering on the edge, his arms wrapped tightly around his chest. As Shadlok uncovered more of the body the shrieks from the mist grew louder, but the fay's magic was powerful, the mist seethed against an invisible barrier, unable to reach the grave.

Something moved on the edge of the clearing. William turned and saw a stag. It sniffed the air and its flanks quivered nervously as it looked around. It took a cautious step forward and turned its dark eyes towards the grave. A second deer, a doe, stepped out of the undergrowth, followed a moment later by a large dog fox.

William stared around the clearing in wonder as squirrels and badgers, a whole family of foxes and several more deer crept out of the forest. One of the fox cubs ran over to the edge of the grave, more curious than fearful. Behind the animals, other creatures emerged from the dusk; strange creatures from hidden places, fays and misty spirit shapes, some no more than tiny points of light, others almost as tall as the trees. They were drawn to the angel like cold hands to a fire.

William looked back at the grave. The angel lay on its back with its hands crossed on its chest. Between its fingers William could see the broken shaft of an arrow, but there was no blood on its robe. Perhaps angels did not have blood. He held his breath as Shadlok carefully brushed the earth from the angel's face with his fingertips.

The creature in the grave might simply have been asleep. The face was long and narrow, with high cheekbones. The smooth skin had a blue tinge, which darkened around the eye sockets and around the nails. Its hair was long and silver-blue and it wore a robe of milk-white fabric, pure and unstained. It was impossible to guess if the creature was male or female; it could have been either.

Suddenly, something deathly cold touched William's leg. He gasped with the shock and stared in horror. They grey mist had broken through Shadlok's barrier and was beginning to climb slowly up his body. Shadlok was still murmuring but his face was twisted with pain and there were beads of sweat on his brow. The mist curled around William like coils of rope, tighter and tighter, higher and higher, slowly crushing the life out of him. He struggled to breathe. Lights whirled inside his head and he felt himself pitching forward into darkness.

And then the grip eased. Cold air flooded into his lungs and he lay gasping and coughing on the ground. He pushed himself up onto his knees and peered around the clearing. The mist had gone. Shadlok had recovered his strength and stood by the grave, arms raised, lips moving soundlessly. The animals stood their ground, eyes wary and bodies tensed for flight.

'Pull the arrow out,' Shadlok said over his shoulder.

It was a moment or so before William realised what the fay meant.

'M . . . me?'

'Do it,' Shadlok snapped.

'Only you can do this, William,' Jacobus called urgently. 'Do it *now*.'

William took a hesitant step towards the edge of the grave. The palms of his clenched hands were damp with sweat and his legs trembled. This was why they had brought him here, he realised. Not to dig up the grave, but to pull the arrow from the angel's body.

'Do what he asks and I will kill you where you stand,' a soft voice said somewhere close by.

William spun around and saw a man dressed all in

263

dark green, standing unarmed and alone at the top of the slope. He heard Shadlok draw a sharp breath. The man was half a head taller than William, lean in build but wide-shouldered. His hair was the colour of old blood and it hung straight and gleaming down his back. His face was sharply boned and his skin was pale and flawless. The shocking brilliance of his green eyes marked him as a creature that was not human. For some reason William knew with complete certainty that this was the Dark King.

'Ignore him. Pull out the arrow,' Shadlok said evenly, glancing down at William. 'Trust me, I will protect you.' He sounded calm but William saw the tense set of his jaw and knew that they were in danger.

'*Do it!*'

William jumped into the grave and knelt down. Carefully, he lifted the angel's hands aside. He gasped as something hit his shoulder and landed on the angel's chest. It was a moment before he realised what it was. A sparrow, small and crumpled, blood gleaming wetly around its open beak. Startled, William fell back against the side of the grave. Seconds later another bird, a robin, landed with a small thud beside the sparrow. It looked as if it had been crushed to death.

The Dark King walked down into the Hollow and stood in front of Shadlok. His eyes burned like wildfire and his mouth was drawn back in a twisted sneer.

'Still surrounding yourself with humans, Sceathhlakk? Have you no pride left?'

Shadlok said nothing. His eyes were slits of blue ice.

The king glanced at William, a look of contempt on his thin face. 'Get away from there.'

William looked uncertainly at Shadlok.

'Remove the arrow, human,' Shadlok said without turning around. 'Do not stop for anything.'

William picked up the dead robin and stroked its chest feathers with a trembling finger. He laid it gently on the edge of the grave and placed the sparrow beside it. He glanced at the Dark King with deep loathing. He was sure the king had killed the birds, using fay magic. But why? The birds had nothing to do with what was happening in the Hollow.

'*The arrow*!' Shadlok said furiously

William bent towards the angel's chest. A high-pitched yowl somewhere close by made him jump. He stared around wildly and saw the dog fox over by the edge of the pond, writhing on the ground in agony. Its legs jerked and its muzzle was flecked with spittle and blood. Its eyes had rolled back in their sockets and were blind white. William watched in horror as the animal fell into the water and struggled desperately to stop itself from drowning.

'Get away from the grave,' the Dark King said, his voice low and full of poison, 'or the blood of every one of these creatures will be on your hands.'

William looked around the Hollow. All the creatures that had come out of the forest were like flies trapped in honey by the king's spell. He saw the glint of terror in wild eyes and the twitch of paralysed bodies. The stag fell to its knees and collapsed onto its side, its mighty antlers gouging the ground as it thrashed in its death throes. With a sudden jerk, its neck broke and the light left its eyes.

William thought he was going to be sick. Bile stung his throat. He slumped forward and touched the cold hand of the angel. There was a tingle in his fingers and he had the oddest sensation of something flowing up into his arm, something calm and pure. He breathed in deeply and straightened up. The Dark King and Shadlok faced each other, eyes locked, bodies rigid. William could feel the magic in the air, heavy and oppressive, as the two fays struggled silently against one another. For a few moments time seemed to stop. They seemed to be equally matched and William felt a brief flicker of relief. If Shadlok could just hold off the king for a few minutes longer . . .

Suddenly, a tangle of black feathers and claws flew across the clearing, heading straight for Shadlok's face. The fay ducked aside and the bird fell to the ground, broken and dead. That brief moment of distraction was all the Dark King needed. He pointed to Shadlok and spoke in a language William did not understand, his words battering Shadlok like sharp stones. Shadlok staggered sideways but quickly regained his footing. He held up a hand as if to shield himself from the king's words but, in the next moment, another crow was hurled through the air and this time its beak and claws caught Shadlock's face. Blood welled from deep gashes on his cheek and trickled down his neck. Then a third crow came flying towards him and, finally shaken into action, William grabbed a stone from the pile of earth beside the grave and flung it as hard as he could, catching the huge bird full on the chest. The crow spun away and landed with a thump on the ground. William desperately hoped it had been dead before his stone hit it.

With a great effort, Shadlok turned and swung his

arm in a wide arc towards the king. Magic crackled through the Hollow like lightning and the Dark King snarled in fury as his words of power fell short of their mark.

Time was running out. William knew he had to pull out the arrow *now*. He forced himself to look away as the fox cub jerked and twitched in a slow and painful death dance. It tumbled into the grave by the angel's head and lay still on the silver-blue hair. William could smell blood and fear on the air and tried to block out the anguished yelps and screams of dying creatures as the enraged king renewed his assault.

Feeling as if his heart was breaking into pieces, William gently pushed the cub's body aside. Taking a deep breath, he gripped the broken arrow shaft and began to pull.

At first, the arrow seemed to be firmly lodged in the angel's chest. Then, slowly, it started to move. William clamped his jaws tightly together and tried not to hear the rasp of wood against flesh and bone as he worked it loose. It came free with a sudden unpleasant slurch and he fell against the side of the grave.

To his horror, the angel's body began to convulse and there was a choking sound in its throat.

William scrambled to his feet, terror shooting

through him like nails. He watched, wide-eyed with disbelief, as the angel put a hand over the wound in its chest. Its mouth opened and it took a huge, juddering breath, gulping at the air, like a drowning man breaking the surface of the water. The eyes opened, black as polished jet, and stared up at the sky.

William edged his way backwards, up and out of the grave. The angel sat up, blinked and gazed around as if it was struggling to understand what was happening. William caught a glimpse of something just showing above its shoulders, the upper curves of white-feathered wings.

The angel rose to its feet slowly and stiffly, as if every joint and muscle hurt, until it was standing upright in the grave, its slim body almost twice William's height. There was a soft rustle as it flexed its wings. They lifted and spread wide, shaking bits of earth and small stones from between the feathers.

The angel turned to look at the two fays. It raised an arm and held the palm of its hand towards the Dark King. For several moments, the king held his ground, the fierce green eyes staring defiantly at the angel, but then his gaze wavered and he took a step backwards. A look of fear briefly weakened the sharp lines of his face.

'It is not over,' he spat, glaring at Shadlok. 'You will pay for this.' And just as suddenly as he arrived he was gone.

Bewildered, William stared at the empty patch of earth where a moment ago the king had been standing. He looked around the clearing but the fay had vanished.

Shadlok walked towards the angel. He knelt beside the grave and bowed his head. His silver-white hair spilled forward and hung down over his chest. The angel leant forward slowly and touched him on the forehead. It looked very like the blessing Prior Ardo gave to his monks.

Looking up at the angel, Shadlok started to speak. William did not understand what he was saying, but the angel clearly did. It listened with an intent expression before turning its dark eyes to Jacobus. It stretched out a hand and beckoned to him with a slow curl of its long fingers.

'Help me, boy,' Jacobus said in a harsh whisper, the mask jerking around to face William.

With great reluctance, William crossed the clearing to Master Bone's side.

'Let me lean on you,' Jacobus said, lifting his arm.

William hesitated, not wanting to touch him. He

forced himself not to pull away when Jacobus rested the stump of his hand on his shoulder. Together they walked towards the angel.

Shadlok got to his feet. He moved aside to allow Jacobus to stand in front of the angel. Jacobus leant more heavily on William, forcing him to stay by his side.

'I beg you to show mercy,' Jacobus said, a break in his voice. 'Set aside the curse that has been placed on me. Let me die.'

William stared at Jacobus. So he was not looking for a cure at all; he wanted death.

'I am begging you,' Jacobus said. He held up his arms and his sleeves fell back, exposing what was left of his hands.

William could not begin to imagine the depths of Master Bone's despair if all he craved now was to be allowed to die.

'Step away, human,' Shadlok said softly.

William took a few steps backwards, until he was standing beside Shadlok.

The angel's black eyes reflected the sparse snowflakes as it looked down at Jacobus. It lifted a hand and pointed to his mask.

Using what was left of a finger, Jacobus pushed

back his hood and pulled down the mask.

William gasped. Master Bone's face hardly merited the name. Where the nose should have been, there was an open wound, wet and dark. His lips had gone, as had his ears. His teeth were black and his skin blotched with weeping sores. Only his brown eyes looked recognisably human. They were wide and clear and filled with despair. It was a terrible sight, like something from a nightmare, and in that moment, William understood what had brought Jacobus to this clearing to beg for death.

The angel did not show any trace of pity or revulsion. There was just a look of infinite compassion on its calm and beautiful face. It leant down and laid a hand on Jacobus's scabbed scalp. Its lips moved soundlessly. Jacobus gave a long shuddering sigh and sank slowly to the ground. His thin body seemed to fold in on itself as he fell sideways and lay still.

A flurry of snowflakes whirled cross the clearing. The angel stepped out of the grave. A wisp of white mist coiled up from the body on the ground. William watched in astonishment as the mist clouded and sharpened, and a man stood there. At first, he was just a pale ghost form, but then colours darkened and details became clearer. The man was tall and lean of build, with dark hair hanging to his shoulders and wide hazel-brown eyes. It was Jacobus Bone, but Jacobus as he had been a long time ago, not the decaying shell he had become. He held up his hands and stared at the long unblemished fingers in wonder, his face shining with fierce joy.

The young Jacobus turned to Shadlok. 'Goodbye, my old friend. Our journey together ends here, but I could never have come this far without you.' He looked at William. 'And my heartfelt gratitude to you, boy. Without you, the king's curse could not have been broken.'

With that, Jacobus bowed to the angel, then turned and walked up the slope and away from the Hollow. He disappeared into the forest without looking back.

The snow was falling more heavily now. It settled on the ground and balanced delicately along branches and twigs. William was too lost in awe of the scene before him to notice the cold.

A softly shimmering light flickered over the angel's body. For a panic-ridden moment William thought it was on fire. He glanced at Shadlok but the fay did not look alarmed. The light grew brighter until it hurt his eyes and he turned away. Then suddenly, the light faded away. It was some moments before his eyes

273

adjusted and he could see the clearing again. The angel had gone.

William knelt down by the grave and picked up the fox cub. He cradled it against his chest, stroking its fur with his thumb. His throat hurt with the effort of not crying. He walked over to the pond and laid the cub gently on the ground. Balancing on a mat of reeds, he reached out to grab the dog fox, to pull it out of the water. His fingers touched wet fur but he couldn't get a hold on the fox's body.

'Step aside,' Shadlok said.

William watched as the fay guided the animal's body to the shore with a branch. When it reached the reeds, Shadlok leant down and lifted it from the pond. It hung limp and dripping in his arms and he laid it down beside the cub.

'Why did he do this?' William asked, his voice thick with tears. 'Why them? They did nothing wrong.'

'He did it to punish you for helping Bone to die,' Shadlok said, his voice surprisingly gentle.

'I hate him.'

'So do I.' Shadlok put a hand on William's shoulder in a brief gesture of sympathy.

William gathered all the bodies together beside the foxes. The stag was too big and heavy to move so he carefully straightened its head on its broken neck.

The snow settled on the still-warm creatures. William crouched down beside them and a hot tear trickled down to his chin and dropped onto the ruffled fur of the cub. William closed his eyes. He wanted to say a prayer, but no words came.

A warm breeze touched his face, and startled, he opened his eyes. Something nudged his leg and he looked down to see the fox cub wriggling to its feet. Too amazed to move, William watched as one by one, the bodies of the dog fox, the crows and the smaller birds struggled back to life, broken bones mending, drowned lungs filling with air. There was a snort and a grunt as the stag scrabbled onto its feet. It stood there trembling, its breath clouding around its head, very much alive.

William started to laugh. He gave a whoop of joy and the stag, startled by the noise, leapt up the slope of the Hollow and back to the safety of the forest.

Quickly and silently, all the animals and fays slipped back to the woods, leaving only their tracks in the snow to show they had ever been there at all.

William and Shadlok faced each other silently for several moments, then Shadlok leant down and lifted Jacobus's body onto his shoulders. He set off up the slope, back to the track and the horses. William followed and stopped for a moment when he reached the trees. A light wind sent snow dancing and whirling through the Hollow. Huge soft flakes settled on the ground around the empty grave. William was not sure if it was his imagination, but the atmosphere in the clearing seemed to have changed. It did not feel so hostile. The air felt lighter and fresher, as if the snow-laden wind had blown away the ancient presence lurking there. Pulling his jacket more tightly around his body, William turned and hurried after Shadlok.

Chapter Twenty-Six

When William reached the trackway, Shadlok was waiting for him. He had slung Master Bone's body over the back of his horse, and stood holding the reins of all three horses. Snowflakes dusted Master Bone's cloak.

'Are we still going to Weforde?' William asked.

'No. We will take Bone's body back to the abbey,' Shadlok replied, handing him Matilda's reins. 'I am sure the monks will not begrudge him burial.'

They walked along without talking for a while. William could see Shadlok's face in the dusk and something in the set of the fay's jaw told him he would be wise to keep silent, but there were things he needed to ask.

'How did you know the angel could overturn the Dark King's curse?'

Shadlok glared at him. 'Do you *ever* stop talking?'

'I helped you tonight. You owe me an explanation.'

The fay sighed heavily. 'There are tales amongst the fay of creatures who pass freely amongst the stars, who were already ancient when this world was new. They have the dust of creation on their feet.' He turned to look at William. 'They have many names, angel is but one of them. They have the power over life and death itself, so it is said. They are the only creatures other than the Creator who could undo the Dark King's curse of eternal life on Jacobus Bone. For many centuries Bone and I searched for them in vain. We finally came across a book in an abbey in France eighty-two winters ago, with pictures of the death of just such a creature, but we knew it could not die. We set out to find its grave and our journey brought us to Crowfield Abbey. The rest of the story you know.'

William shivered. What if Shadlok and Master Bone had not discovered the book in the French abbey? Would the angel have lain in the earth until Judgement Day? There were so many questions and no answers, just mysteries wrapped inside puzzles, like the layers of an onion, one inside another.

'What about Brother Snail?' William asked at last.

'The monk is unharmed,' Shadlok said.

'So he'll wake up now?'

Shadlok's eyes narrowed. 'You doubt me?'

William shrugged.

The fay stared ahead, his eyes as cold as the snow whirling past his face.

William was uncomfortably aware that he had managed to insult Shadlok. They continued on their way in silence.

There was one last thing William still wanted to know. It had been troubling him since their visit to Dame Alys's house. 'What was the thing in the bird-mask that I saw yesterday?' he asked.

Shadlok glanced at him. 'I believe it was one of the old gods of this land.'

'A god?' William said in surprise. 'But there's only one, isn't there?'

'There is only one Creator,' Shadlok said, nodding, 'but there are many others who have been worshipped as gods, and the thing you saw in the hut is one of them. It inhabited a sacred grove of trees that was cared for by the woman's ancestors. It seems she has not turned her back on the old ways, as so many others have.'

'But what *is* it? Is it a fay, or a demon?' William persisted. 'A ghost, perhaps?'

There was an odd glitter in Shadlok's eyes as he

turned to look at William. 'It is an angel.'

William's stared at Shadlok. 'An *angel*? It can't be.'

'Why not?'

'Because it was evil,' William said.

'Like fays and humans, there are dark and light angels. I believe the angel you saw in the woman's house is a creature of the darkness. The angel we freed from its grave was sent here to hunt it down.'

'That was why Dame Alys never told anyone about the angel,' William said, suddenly understanding. 'She must have known it wasn't really dead and she didn't want anyone to find it, because it would come after *her* angel.'

Shadlok nodded. 'Exactly, and she could not allow that to happen. A word of warning, the woman and the angel she serves are drawn to those whose hearts are good, people like you. Turning *you* from the Creator would matter more to them than you could ever imagine. Stay away from Dame Alys from now on.'

William nodded. He just hoped *she* would stay away from *him*.

Shadlok touched William's arm and nodded towards a stand of birch trees a little way ahead. The thin white trunks were pale stripes against the dark woods. William couldn't see anything to explain the fay's sudden wariness.

'What?' William said, frowning. 'There's nothing there.'

'Look again,' Shadlok said softly. He drew his sword and handed the reins of the two horses to William. 'Stay behind me.'

Peering through the snow, William thought he glimpsed something green move between the trees. Shadlok walked slowly along the track, sword at the ready, until he reached the birches, and then he stopped. William heard him say something but the wind carried the words away.

The horses started to pull at their reins. Matilda whinnied and jerked her head back. The other two danced nervously, eyes rolling and nostrils flaring as fear infected them. William turned his back on Shadlok as he struggled to control the horses.

'Steady!' he said, trying to stroke Matilda's neck, but she was beyond listening to him.

William looked over his shoulder. All he could see of Shadlok was his white hair. In front of him was a blur of green. Was it the Dark King? he wondered anxiously. Had he come to kill Shadlok?

William felt powerless. He couldn't help Shadlok,

and unless he let go of the horses' reins and made a run for it, he couldn't help himself either.

'Hush, Tildy,' he said, desperately trying to calm the horse. The other two tugged at their reins and he had to wrap the thin leather strips around his wrists to stop them slipping out of his grip. He kept a wary eye on the pawing hooves.

Something touched William's shoulder and he turned, half expecting to find a sword blade pointing at his throat. To his surprise, he saw Shadlok standing in front of him, his face tense, his eyes narrowed to icy slits.

'Give me the reins,' the fay said.

William did as he was told. He looked at the stand of birch trees. The patch of green had gone. 'Was that the king?' he asked anxiously.

Shadlok nodded. He whispered something to the three nervous horses, stroking their muzzles and patting their necks. William was astonished to see their ears prick forward as they listened to him. They grew calmer and Matilda nuzzled his shoulder gently.

'He came to tell me that I will be allowed to live for now, and to warn you that he will not forget your part in what happened today.'

William felt sick. How was that fair? 'But I didn't

have a choice in the matter.'

'That means nothing to him,' Shadlok said scornfully. 'The king is cunning and his memory is long, human. Keep your eyes open and your wits about you at all times. He will come for you when you least expect it.'

William gave Matilda's reins a tug and put his head down against the driving snow. Sick dread churned in his stomach. Was Shadlok right? Would the Dark King really come after him, simply because he'd been forced to help dig up the angel? William urged Matilda on. He wouldn't be happy until he was safely inside the abbey walls.

Chapter Twenty-Seven

The snow stopped shortly before dawn. The walls of the abbey were stark and grey against the dazzling brilliance of the garden and sheep pasture as William trudged through the snowdrifts to the infirmary. His breath clouded around his head. A bell rang out, calling the monks to the church for prime. Later that morning, after mass and the daily chapter meeting, Master Bone was to be buried.

William let himself into the infirmary and closed the door behind him quickly, so as not to let the cold air into the room. Not that it would have made a great deal of difference. It was almost as cold inside as it was outside.

Brother Odo was huddled on his stool in front of the altar at the far end of the infirmary, wrapped in a thick woollen cloak. He had his back to the rest of the chamber. He did not turn around or appear to be aware that William was there.

The old monk had placed wooden screens either side of Brother Snail's bed to block draughts and hold in the warmth from the brazier. Apple wood smoke scented the air and drifted up to the rafters.

William stood beside Snail's bed. The monk was lying curled over on his side, with one hand under his chin, snoring softly. There was a faint flush of colour in his cheeks. William looked down at him for a few moments, and then reached out and gently shook his shoulder.

'Brother Snail?' he said.

The monk's eyelids fluttered and opened. The blue eyes gazed vaguely around and settled on William.

'Will, how good to see you, lad.' His voice was weak but his smile was wide.

William grinned back, hugely relieved.

There was a scrabbling in the straw beneath the bed and the hob appeared. He climbed up to sit beside the monk. His fur was sleek and as glossy as a chestnut. It seemed the hob had passed the time grooming himself. His tail curled over Brother Snail's shoulder.

'The snail brother started to wake at dusk yesterday. I gave him some water.' The hob patted Snail's cheek with a small, leathery paw. 'He is much better now.'

William sat on the edge of the bed, his chest swelling with happiness to see his friend none the worse for Shadlok's spell.

'Brother Walter tells me Master Bone is dead,' Snail whispered. 'What happened, Will?'

William told the monk and the hob everything that had happened in the Hollow. They listened in silence.

'You found the angel,' Brother Snail said, a look of elation in his eyes, 'and it is *alive*. Will, that is wonder-ful! A miracle.'

William nodded, smiling at the monk's obvious delight.

'How I envy you, seeing such a thing. And its wings? What did they look like?' There was an almost childlike excitement in Brother Snail's voice.

'They reached from its shoulders to its feet, and were as white as swans' wings,' William said.

'How beautiful,' Brother Snail sighed. 'You are truly fortunate to have seen it for yourself.' A little of the light left his eyes. 'I am sorry for Master Bone, but I think he must have suffered terribly all these years. He is at peace now.'

William stood up. He was reluctant to leave but he still had a day's work ahead of him. 'I'll come and see you later, and bring you some food.' He saw the expectant look on the hob's face and grinned. 'Both of you.'

'Don't trouble yourself, Will,' Brother Snail said, struggling to sit up. William reached out to help him, and wrapped a blanket around the monk's bowed back. 'I am feeling much better and I have work to do, potions and salves to prepare against winter chills and aches.'

'You should stay here,' William said. 'It's a bitter day and you need to get your strength back.'

'If I waited for that to happen, I'd never leave my bed,' Snail said wryly. 'No, I'll be all right, Will, and I have Brother Walter to help me.'

William knew it was pointless to argue with the monk. He could be very stubborn when he wanted. 'Very well, but I'll bring some bread and cheese and warm milk to the workshop.'

William pulled on his mittens and walked to the door. The hob scurried after him.

'Is the forest safe again? Do you think the nangel will guard it against the Dark King and his followers?' the hob asked, the bright green-gold eyes searching William's face for reassurance.

William's heart sank. Did the hob want to return to Foxwist? Now that his leg was better, there was no reason for him to stay at the abbey. He would miss him sorely.

'As safe as it can ever be, but I don't know if the angel will stay to watch over it,' he said.

A worried look puckered the hob's small face. 'Do I *have* to go back to the woods?' he asked, the words tumbling out in a rush.

William smiled. 'Not if you don't want to.'

'The snail brother needs me to help him, and the old pig asked me to keep her company sometimes . . .' the hob hurried on, his paws twisting together and his tail curling and flicking straight in his anxiety to convince William of his need to stay at Crowfield.

'You are welcome to stay for as long as you want,' William said gently. 'I want you to stay.'

'Then I will,' the hob said, sounding more cheerful.

Brother Walter went back to Brother Snail's bed and William could hear the two of them talking quietly.

In the distance, the bell for mass tolled. It was almost time to bury Master Bone.

Chapter Twenty-Eight

A few flakes of snow drifted down and settled on the dark earth heaped up beside the newly dug grave. A small plot in a neglected corner of the graveyard was all Prior Ardo had been willing to spare for Master Bone. It was well away from the monks' graves. Even in death, it seemed Jacobus the leper was to be shunned.

William leant on the handle of his shovel and watched Peter push the handcart containing Jacobus Bone's shrouded body along the path. The wooden cartwheels left deep ruts in the snow. Prior Ardo, Brother Gabriel and Shadlok followed a short distance behind him. The prior's murmured prayer for the dead was the only sound in the wintry stillness.

Peter stopped beside the grave and set the props of the handcart down.

'Can you help me lift him?' he asked, turning to William.

William nodded. Together, they lifted the body from the cart and carried it to the edge of the grave. The grave was shallow, little more than knee-deep. William clambered awkwardly into the hole, while struggling to keep hold of Jacobus's feet. Wiry roots caught at his legs and snagged on the tightly-wrapped folds of the shroud, which was really an old linen altar cloth, much patched and faded from years of use and no longer wanted. Peter stepped into the other end of the grave. There was just enough room for them to brace their feet against the sides of the hole and lower the body.

William climbed out and wiped his hands on his trouser legs. Jacobus's body had been surprisingly light, but his flesh had felt unpleasantly soft and cold through the thin linen.

William picked up a shovel. He glanced at Shadlok. The fay was staring down at the body of his former master, his face expressionless. The dark tunic and cloak he wore made his skin and hair look eerily pale in the harsh winter light. The cuts on his cheek were dark, ugly weals. If he felt any grief at Jacobus's death, he gave no sign of it. William started to shovel the earth into the grave.

The prior crossed himself and tucked his bony hands into the sleeve of his habit. 'Come to the chapter house as soon as you've finished here, boy,' he said, looking at William. 'I want to talk to you.'

William nodded, surprised by the unexpected request. Prior Ardo turned and walked away, followed by Peter and Brother Gabriel.

'I wonder what he wants with me?' William said with a frown.

There was a trace of impatience in the look Shadlok gave him. 'Go and find out.'

When the last shovelful of earth had been patted into place, William pulled on his mittens and trudged back through the snow to the abbey. He glanced over his shoulder when he reached the passageway to the cloisters. Shadlok was standing beside the grave, staring into the distance. There was a look of such bleak despair on his face that William hesitated for a moment. Should he go back and say something to try and comfort him? But what could he say?

Shadlok wrapped his cloak closely about him and walked away, and the moment was lost. William went on his way, his heart heavy with pity.

The chapter house door was open. William hesitated on the threshold. He had never been allowed in here before. When it needed to be swept and the cobwebs brushed from the corners, Peter did it.

He knocked on the heavy oak door.

'Come in,' Prior Ardo called.

William stepped inside and glanced around curiously. The chamber had a high vaulted ceiling and the floor was patterned with red and white tiles. There was a tall arched window high up in the east wall, in the centre of which stood the Archangel Michael, made from small pieces of coloured glass set in a web of lead strips. A warrior angel, dressed for battle, wings spread wide behind him. Yellow hair curled around his face, and a golden halo ringed his head. He wore a breastplate over a chain mail tunic and held a sword above his head. One foot rested on the neck of a dead dragon and there was a look of triumph on his face.

On either side of the window the walls had been painted with robed figures. William had no idea who they were supposed to be, apart from one tucked into a gloomy corner of the room. That one had outstretched wings too, but with its curly brown hair and plump pink face, it looked nothing like the angel in the Hollow or the dragon-slaying warrior in the east window.

William noticed that someone had drawn a feather to one side of the angel's head. William suspected it had been drawn as a reminder to each successive abbot of Crowfield's dark secret.

There were ornate stone niches around the walls for the monks to sit in. One seat was grander than the rest. The carved canopy was painted red and gold. It took the place of honour in the wall opposite the door. This was, he guessed, the abbot's seat, but today, Prior Ardo sat in it. There was a large oak table in front of him. On it lay a long, narrow leather bag.

'Come forward, boy, where I can see you.'

William did as he was told. He pushed back his hood and stood awkwardly in front of the table, ill at ease beneath the prior's brooding stare. The snow on his boots melted into puddles around his feet.

Prior Ardo reached forward and pushed the leather bag across the table towards him. 'Master Bone asked me to give this to you in the event of his death.'

Startled, William picked up the bag and pulled open the drawstring. He took out Master Bone's wooden flute. He looked up at the prior, instinctively trying to hide his delight. He saw the prior's disapproving frown and put the flute back in its bag.

'I don't know why he left it to you, though I am sure

he had his reasons, but I do not want to hear you play that instrument in the abbey,' the prior said. He waved a dismissive hand at William. 'Now go about your duties.'

William hugged the bag to his chest. Any fears he might have had at owning a leper's flute were far outweighed by his gratitude to Master Bone and his sudden burning excitement at the thought of one day being able to play the instrument.

As William turned to leave, Brother Gabriel burst into the room, slamming the heavy door back against the wall. His plump face was scarlet and he gasped like a fish on a riverbank. William's first thought was that the monk was ill. The prior got to his feet and hurried around the table towards him, a look of alarm on his face, but Brother Gabriel held up a hand and crouched forward for a moment as he tried to catch his breath.

'Come . . . quick . . . ly,' he panted, 'Abbot . . . Simon . . .'

Prior Ardo did not wait for him to finish. He was out of the room at a run. Brother Gabriel lowered himself onto one of the stone seats around the wall and sat there, hands on knees, drops of sweat beading his flushed face and the shaved circle of the tonsure on top of his head, breathing wheezily.

'Is the abbot dead?' William asked.

Brother Gabriel shook his head. 'No. He is awake and asking to be taken down to the church, and he told me to fetch the . . .' The monk's mouth closed like a trap, biting off the last word. The colour in his cheeks darkened a shade or two and he looked away. 'Nothing.'

'He asked you to fetch nothing?' William said, baffled by the monk's odd behaviour.

'It is none of your concern, boy,' Brother Gabriel said sharply. 'Go to the barn and fetch a fence hurdle and bring it to Abbot Simon's quarters. And hurry!'

William stared at the monk, bewildered. A fence hurdle?

'Go on, boy, run!' Brother Gabriel snapped. He dabbed at his sweaty face with the sleeve of his habit and struggled to his feet. 'If you see Brother Stephen in the yard, tell him he is needed here.'

Tucking the flute into the front of his tunic, William did as he was told. He could see several monks on the far side of the cloister garth, gathered outside the doorway of the abbot's quarters. He heard anxious voices and sensed their agitation. He thought of the abbot, lying close to death in his bed these last weeks, and wondered how the frail old man had rallied sufficiently to ask to be taken to the church. And what had he asked Brother Gabriel to fetch? Was it, by any chance, the angel's feather?

William went out to the yard through the kitchen door. The drift of snow that had piled up against the outside of the door collapsed across the floor. He stepped over it and headed across the yard towards the small barn. The snow was ankle-deep in places, but knee-deep where it had been blown against walls, or had slid from rooftops to land in huge soft heaps. It worked its way inside his boots and melted there, quickly soaking the feet of his hose.

Brother Stephen had cleared a patch of ground around the pig and goat pens. The doorway of the hen house was still closed, with the hens safe and warm inside, though the monk had cleared a narrow path to it so he could feed them. Of the monk himself, there was no sign.

The small barn was used to store barley and oats, and it was in here that Brother Stephen kept the fence hurdles that he, William and Peter wove from hazel withies cut in the coppice in Foxwist early in the autumn. The hurdles were good and sturdy, and would be used to replace sections of old and rotten fencing around the sheep pasture. William hauled one from the stack against the barn wall and, twisting his fingers between the withies, lifted it and carried it out to the yard.

'What do you want with that, Will?'

William turned and saw Brother Stephen, his thin face reddened by the cold wind, standing in the doorway of the carpentry shed, hands on hips and sawdust on his habit.

William explained briefly. The monk's mouth tightened and he merely nodded when William finished. Never one to waste words, he closed the shed door behind him and hurried over to take one end of the hurdle from William. Between them, they carried it back to the abbey and up to the abbot's quarters.

The bedchamber was crowded with monks, most of them praying and getting in each other's way. The abbot lay amongst the blankets and coverlets heaped on the bed. There were patches of feverish colour on his cheeks, and his rheumy eyes in their shadow-ringed sockets were open. He gaze settled on William and he watched him with an intensity that William found unsettling.

'Put the hurdle here,' Prior Ardo said, pointing to the floor beside the bed.

William watched as Brother Gabriel dragged a sheepskin cover from the bed and put it on the hurdle, and then put a folded blanket on top of it. The prior pulled back the abbot's covers and with great care, slipped his arms under the old monk's body and lifted him up. Silence fell in the chamber as the prior gently laid the abbot on the hurdle and settled him comfortably. William held his breath and wondered how a body that was no more than a bundle of bones held together with skin as fragile as old parchment could still cling to life.

The prior tucked blankets around the abbot and eased a down-filled pillow beneath his head. He looked over his shoulder at William and Brother Stephen.

'Carry our father down to the church.'

William took the foot of the hurdle, while Brother Stephen took the head, and together, they lifted it off the floor and carried it to the doorway. William saw that the abbot was still staring at him. The old man's lips moved but William could not hear his whispered words. Prior Ardo leant down and put his ear close to the abbot's mouth, a puzzled frown on his face. He glanced up at William and the frown deepened.

'Abbot Simon wants me to tell you . . .' he began,

then paused. 'He said, "Tell the boy to beware the coming darkness." He said, "The light shines brightly in this boy, and it marks him out from his fellows. His path will not be an easy one but he will not walk it alone."'

All eyes turned to stare at William. He felt himself redden under the weight of their curiosity.

'What does that mean?' Brother Gabriel whispered, looking from the prior to William and back again, his plump face perplexed.

Looks of mingled unease and suspicion went between the monks in the room. William could almost feel them pull away from him as if he was something dangerous. Only Brother Snail stood his ground, his frail, hunched body huddled inside his cloak. He smiled at William and there was a look of compassion in his eyes as if he understood just how alone William felt at that moment.

Perhaps they're wise to be wary of me, William thought. *I have the Sight; I walked away from a fire that should have burned me to death; and I was chosen by a cursed man and a fay to release an angel from a dark and evil spell. The abbot is right; I'm marked out from the people around me.*

'What does our father mean,' Brother Gabriel

continued, a quiver in his voice, 'the coming darkness? What darkness would that be?'

'I don't know.' Prior Ardo regarded William thoughtfully, as if seeing him for the first time. 'But it can wait for now. We must get Abbot Simon to the church.'

Brother Martin and Brother Gabriel went on ahead down the narrow stairs. William and Brother Stephen followed, one slow, awkward step at a time, trying not to tip the hurdle too much in case the abbot rolled off.

William puzzled over the abbot's words. What did the abbot mean by the darkness? Did he mean the Dark King? But how could the bedridden old man possibly know anything about *him*? No, William thought, the abbot had said the *coming* darkness. Whatever it was, it hadn't happened yet. A feeling of foreboding passed over him like a cold shadow.

'Have a care, boy!' Brother Stephen said sharply. William had not been paying full attention to what he was doing and he had trapped the monk's hand between the edge of the hurdle and the wall.

'Sorry,' William muttered.

'Yes, well, don't do it again.'

They reached the foot of the staircase and angled the hurdle out into the cloister alley. It was snowing again. A restless wind sent flakes whirling across the cloister garth and through the arched openings of the north alley. William put his head down against the wind as the icy snowflakes stung his face and briefly blinded him. It was a relief when they reached the door into the south aisle of the church and went inside the building.

A pile of snow lay on the nave floor beneath the hole in the roof. Prior Ardo stared at it, momentarily distracted from the task in hand. He glanced up at a patch of white sky between the bare roof timbers and his face hardened into its habitual lines of weary resignation. It was just one more thing he would have to see to.

William and Brother Stephen carried the abbot into the chancel. Brother Snail and Brother Mark hurried to collect as many lanterns, candlesticks and wax and tallow candles as they could find. They put them on the chancel floor, the altar and in brackets on the choir stalls. Brother Odo followed along behind, lighting them with a taper. The flames glowed like little white stars in the gloom.

'Put the hurdle here,' the prior said, pointing to the floor in front of the steps up to the high altar. For a moment William hesitated. The abbot's covers would not keep out the biting chill and draughts that cut across the tiled floor. Then he thought, *does it matter?* The old man was as close to death as it was possible to be.

William stepped back from the hurdle. Someone touched his arm. He looked around and saw Brother Snail. The monk gestured for him to stand over by the choir stalls.

The monks took their places in the stalls and began to sing. The Latin words of a psalm rose into the darkness above the shimmering haze from the candle flames. At a nod from the prior, Brother Gabriel slipped away from his stall and returned several minutes later carrying a wooden box. As he passed by, William saw that it was the box from the sacristy cupboard, the one in which the feather was kept. The monk carried it over to Prior Ardo and William watched as the prior lifted the lid.

There were one or two wary glances in William's direction from the other monks, as if they were not sure that he should be watching this. William ignored them. He had as much right here as any of them. After all, he was the only person in the church who had ever actually seen the angel.

There was a collective gasp as the prior carefully

lifted the feather from the box and held it up. It gleamed with a soft radiance in the candlelight. He knelt beside the abbot and laid the feather on the old monk's chest.

With an effort, the abbot freed one hand from beneath the covers and his thin fingers clutched the feather. William thought he saw a smile lift the corners of the old man's mouth.

William noticed a small point of light near the east wall. At first he thought it was a reflection off the silver crucifix on the altar, but after staring at it for a couple of moments, William realised the light was hovering somewhere between the altar and the dying abbot. His scalp prickled uneasily as he watched the light begin to move slowly down the chancel.

The singing faltered and faded away as one by one the monks saw the light, until the only sound was the fitful gusting of the wind outside the church. William glanced around and saw fear in the eyes of the monks nearest to him. Peter Borowe, standing on the far side of the chancel, stared at the light with a look of wonder on his face. His mouth widened into a smile and he clapped his hands together softly.

The candle flames in the chancel guttered in the draughts. The painted faces of saints were briefly illuminated before shadows wavered across the walls and hid them again.

The light became steadily brighter. It reached the foot of the abbot's hurdle and stopped. William held his breath and watched as the light began to grow in size, spreading downwards until it touched the floor, and upwards to the roof beams. It took on the shape of a human body, filling the chancel with a dazzling white glare that hurt William's eyes. The terrified monks huddled in their stalls, praying aloud. The prior crouched beside the abbot, his thin arms covering the old man's body as if to protect him.

Gradually, the light eased and lost its painfully bright intensity. Blind spots swam in front of William's eyes but he could just make out a huge glowing figure, arms spread wide. Blue fire shimmered around it like a halo. Light radiated from its face, so that all William could see of its features were shadows where the eyes should have been. Its hair hung over its shoulders and shone like molten silver. In one outstretched hand it held a sword with a golden blade. From its back, two feathered wings spread out, their pointed tips almost touching the floor tiles.

The angel bore little resemblance to the one in the Hollow, but William knew with a deep certainty that it was the same creature, just as he felt sure that this was closer to its true shape: a being of light that filled him with a bewildering mixture of bone-melting fear and a joy so profound it hurt.

The prior knelt beside the hurdle, his whole body shaking, his hands clasped together tightly in prayer. His head was bowed and his eyes squeezed shut.

William watched as Abbot Simon struggled to sit up and push aside his coverlets. He was still holding the feather and he seemed to be drawing strength from the angel. His face was lit with a radiance that was startling to witness. Tears trickled down his sunken cheeks and his eyes seemed to stare beyond the walls of the church at something only he could see. Without stopping to think, William darted forward and helped Abbot Simon to his feet. He put an arm around the old monk's waist to support him.

A wave of painfully brilliant light billowed out from the angel. It lit up the inside of William's skull, and for a few moments he could not move. Then, just as suddenly, the light was gone and the abbot slumped in his arms. Shaking with fright, William lowered the abbot's body to the floor. He knew the monk was dead.

Prior Ardo hurried over to kneel beside the abbot. He

crossed the abbot's arms on his chest and straightened his linen tunic around his legs. William looked around for the feather, thinking that the abbot had dropped it, but it was nowhere to be seen.

'The feather,' he said, looking at the prior, 'it's gone.'

The prior glanced at him with a quick frown and turned his attention back to the abbot.

William stood up and gazed around the chancel. There was nothing to show that the angel had been there but something had changed inside the church. Or maybe, William thought, the church is just the same as always, but *I've* changed. He felt stronger, calmer. The hardships and the losses of his past no longer mattered. It was as if he had spent his life peering at the ground and had just looked up and seen the sky for the first time.

Brother Snail came to stand beside him. The monk was smiling and there was a light in his eyes that told William he was feeling the same sense of wonder. He looked up at William and the smile broadened. William grinned back. There was no need for words.

Chapter Twenty-Nine

William stood in the archway to the cloister garth, watching the snow weave complicated patterns against the grey afternoon sky. He hardly noticed the cold. He could hear the monks singing in the church and understood their need to mark what they had just witnessed. For them it was by praying and singing psalms; for William it was standing in the snow and feeling the swirling flakes brush his face with their icy softness. High above the abbey, the slow toll of the passing bell rang out.

William took the flute from inside his tunic. Through the leather bag, he traced the shape of the instrument. His fingers touched the holes along its length as he tried to imagine the music he would one day be able to play on it. He sensed rather than saw Shadlok come to stand beside him.

'What is that?' Shadlok asked.

'It's Master Bone's flute.'

'His flute?' Shadlok's tone was sharp.

William nodded and turned to look at the fay. 'He asked the prior to give it to me.'

Shadlok closed his eyes for a moment and smiled grimly. 'I should have known.'

'What?' William asked, mystified. 'What's wrong?'

'Bone did not leave you the flute.'

'But the prior said . . .'

'I know what he said,' Shadlok said softly. 'But Bone left you his *lute*, not the flute.'

William stared at the fay, feeling as if he had been kicked in the stomach. He half-turned with some idea of going back to the chapter house and asking the prior for what was rightfully his, but then he stopped.

'Prior Ardo will deny it,' he said flatly. 'It'll be our word against his.'

Shadlok said nothing. He folded his arms and turned to look out at the falling snow.

William was torn between resentment at the prior's deceit, and understanding what had made him do it. The lute was a beautiful and valuable instrument. The money the prior could raise from selling it would pay for repairs to the nave roof, or perhaps buy a couple of goats and an extra pig next spring. He looked down at the leather bag in his hand. *Let the prior have the lute,* he thought, *I have something far more precious. I have a future.*

'I'll need to find someone to teach me how to play,' William said. 'One day, I'll leave the abbey and make my way in the world as a musician.'

'I can teach you,' the fay said with a shrug, glancing at him. 'I taught Bone. I can make a musician of you.'

William grinned. 'That will annoy the prior.'

'I know,' Shadlok said with a gleam in his eye. 'Fair payment for his dishonesty, wouldn't you say?'

'Very fair. Does this mean you intend to stay at Crowfield for now?'

Shadlok's mouth tightened into a hard line. 'I have no choice in the matter.'

William frowned at him, puzzled. 'Why?'

It was some moments before the fay spoke. There was a strange expression in his pale-blue eyes when he turned to face William. 'The Dark King put a curse on me a long time ago. It bound me to Jacobus Bone for as long as he lived.'

'Master Bone is dead,' William said. 'Surely now you're free to go wherever you want?'

Shadlok's face twisted with sudden anger.

Snowflakes caught in the silver-white strands of his hair. 'My curse is to have my fate bound to that of a human until such time as the king sees fit to release me, which I very much doubt he ever will. I am no longer bound to Bone, I am bound to *you*.'

'Me?' William gasped. 'Why did he bind you to *me*?'

'He didn't,' Shadlok said. 'When the possibility that Bone might finally die became a reality, *we* chose the next human for me to be bound to. We chose you.'

William stared at him, appalled. That was what Jacobus Bone must have meant yesterday in the Hollow when he said, 'We chose well, my old friend.' The words echoed inside William's mind. He had been like a pig to the slaughter, not seeing the blade at his throat until it was too late.

'You had no right to do that,' William said angrily. He gripped the flute so tightly that his knuckles went white. 'Isn't there some way to break the curse?'

'No. Only your death will free you. You must accept it.' The pale eyes glittered dangerously, daring him to argue.

William felt sick. What if Shadlok grew tired of being bound to him? Would he simply kill him and move on to the next person?

As if guessing what was in William's mind, Shadlok smiled thinly and said, 'I cannot harm the human I am tied to, if that is what you are thinking. It is part of the curse that I have to protect and . . . serve this one person. That was why we had to choose carefully.'

'I'm glad to hear it,' William said with feeling, 'but you must know that it means you'll have to live here at Crowfield as long as I do.' If that didn't force Shadlok to find a way to break the curse, then nothing would.

'I am only too well aware of that,' Shadlok said grimly.

William felt a flicker of gleeful pleasure at the thought of Shadlok rubbing shoulders with the monks of Crowfield Abbey every day, though he realised that his life was never going to be the same again. Wherever he went, whatever he did, this fay warrior would be at his side. He remembered what Abbot Simon had said, that his path would not be an easy one, but that he'd never be alone. Somehow, the dying monk had seen what was ahead of William and had tried to warn him. Only, there was nothing he could do about it. He would simply have to try and make the best of this strange turn of events.

'Have you asked the prior if you can stay at Crowfield?' William asked.

'This morning, before Bone's burial, but why would he refuse?' Shadlok's voice was edged with contempt. 'In return for a bed and two meals a day, which I neither want nor need, I will work from dawn till dusk. The prior knows a bargain when he sees one.'

'What about the rest of Master Bone's possessions? What will happen to them?'

'He left them to the abbey. The prior will most likely sell them along with the lute.'

'I suppose you can't blame him for that,' William said grudgingly.

'I don't. Bone has no further need of them.'

'Then it seems we are stuck with each other,' William said at last. 'If you teach me to play my flute, perhaps one day we can leave Crowfield and travel the world together.'

'The prospect fills me with delight,' Shadlok said scathingly.

William pulled a face. 'You have only yourself to blame, you know. You didn't *have* to choose me.'

'No? Perhaps I should have bound myself to the prior, or one of the other monks. At least you are young and have the Sight, and you are as anxious

to leave this place one day as I am. You have . . .
potential.'

'Does this mean you are now my servant?' William
asked with feigned innocence. The look of outrage on
the fay's face told him he had hit his target squarely
and he laughed.

'Most amusing,' Shadlok said, scowling. He
brushed past William and walked away.

William was still grinning to himself when he set
off to find the hob and Brother Snail, to show them
his flute. Perhaps being bound to Shadlok might not
be so bad after all.

Later that evening, when the monks were in bed and
silence had settled over the abbey, William sat by the
fire in the kitchen, his blanket around his shoulders.
The hob sat beside him, tucked under a corner of the
blanket. William told the hob everything that had
happened that day, from Master Bone's burial to
Shadlok's curse. But it was the appearance of the angel
in the church that interested the hob the most, and he
made William tell the story several times before he
was satisfied.

'I am glad the nangel isn't dead,' the hob said
sleepily. He leant against William and settled himself

more comfortably.

'So am I,' William said, nodding. 'I wonder if we'll ever see it again?'

'I didn't see it *this* time,' the hob said. He had been very put out to realise he'd been busy in Brother Snail's workshop when the angel had come to take the abbot's soul away.

William yawned loudly and stretched his arms above his head. His body ached with tiredness. 'Well, I don't know about you, but I'm ready for my bed.'

The hob curled up on the mattress. 'Nangels and squirrels and snow,' he murmured drowsily, 'magic and shadows, roundy-round, all together.'

William smiled and tucked the blanket around the hob. He lifted the *couvre-feu* and placed it carefully over the fire-pit, then lay down beside the hob and closed his eyes. Within minutes he was in a deep and dreamless sleep.

Winter timetable for daily life at Crowfield Abbey

2.00 am – **vigils,** then reading/praying.

Sunrise – **lauds.**

6.00 am – **prime,** followed by High Mass.

8.00 am – **tierce,** followed by Chapter Meeting.

9.45 am – 12.00pm – work.

12.00 pm – **sext** (if monks are away from abbey, in fields, they stop and pray where they are).

1.00 pm – **nones,** followed by dinner, then into church to give thanks for food and to sing Psalm 31.

2.45 pm – work and time spent in cloister or warming house.

Dusk – **vespers** followed by reading in cloisters, then **compline,** warm drink and to bed.

Glossary of terms

Book of hours: a book of prayers, psalms and holy texts, hand-written and illuminated by monks.

Caudle: a medicinal hot drink for minor ailments, made with wine or ale, thickened with breadcrumbs, egg yolks or ground almonds.

Cellarer/cellarium: the cellarer is the monk in charge of the abbey's provisions and store room, or cellarium.

Cess-pit: a pit for rubbish and/or sewage.

Chapter house: a room off the cloister, close to the south door of the church. The monks meet here each day to discuss abbey business and listen to a reading from the Rule of St Benedict.

Choir: at Crowfield Abbey, this is the area between the transepts and the east end of the church. Two rows of wooden stalls, or seats, face each other across the width of the choir. The monks sit here during the daily round of services.

Cloister: four covered alleys or corridors surrounding a central garden or garth, usually situated on the south side of the abbey church. The main rooms of the abbey can be reached from the cloister.

Dorter/dormitory: the open-plan room on the first floor of the east range of the buildings surrounding the cloisters, where the monks sleep.

Frater: a long room where the monks eat their meals. At Crowfield Abbey, the frater is in the west range, between the kitchens and the guest quarters.

Hurdy-gurdy: a stringed musical instrument. The strings pass over a wheel, which is turned by a crank handle. The wheel acts very much like a violin bow, producing musical notes from the strings. When played, the hurdy-gurdy sounds like a bagpipe.

Maslin bread: made from a mixture of rye and wheat flour. After a poor harvest, dried and ground peas or beans could be added to the flour.

Midden: a rubbish tip.

Mummers: mummers and guisers were street performers in towns and villages, who dressed up and wore masks and entertained people, usually around Christmas. They cavorted around the streets, singing carols and playing music and sometimes begging for money from door to door. Later on, mummers performed plays which included such characters as St George, Beelzebub and Robin Hood.

Nave: the long, main body of the church.

Pannage: the practice of allowing pigs to forage in woodland for beech-mast and acorns from September to early November.

Parchment/vellum: thin sheets of sheep-, goat- or calf-skin used for pages of books or manuscripts. The skin is stretched, scraped and dried to prepare it. Better quality skins are called vellum.

Pottage: a cross between a soup and a stew, usually made with whatever vegetables were available. In winter, dried peas were a staple ingredient. Sometimes a little meat or fish would be included. Herbs such as wild garlic, thyme, rosemary, sage and parsley would be added for flavour and salt for seasoning.

Psalms: religious songs sung or recited as part of daily worship. A book of psalms is a psalter.

Reredorter: the monks' latrines or toilets, situated next to the dorter.

Rushlight: a type of candle, made from rushes. The inner pith of the rush is dipped in fat, grease or beeswax. The pith then acts as the wick when the rushlight is lit.

Sacristy/sacristan: the room where the abbey's more valuable possessions are kept locked away. The sacristan is the monk in charge of the sacristy. At Crowfield Abbey, this is one of Brother Snail's duties.

Shawm: a woodwind instrument, similar to a modern oboe.

Small beer: a diluted beer with a very low alcohol content, drunk by adults and children with meals.

Transepts: the shorter cross-arms of the church, between the nave and the choir.

Acknowledgements

I would like to say a heartfelt thank-you to everyone at the Chicken House, for believing in the book and for all their help and encouragement. I would especially like to thank Imogen Cooper, my editor, and my agent, Linda Davis. There are, of course, many more people who helped the book on its way. Thank you to one and all.

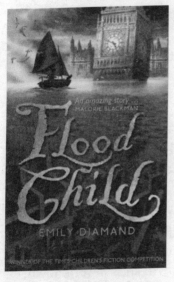

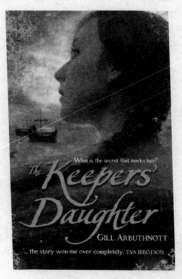